the house, when ...
talk more in the cool light of the morn.
But that moment passed by so quickly
it did not hinder his next action at all.
Tavis pulled her back into his arms,
tilted her head with his hand and
leaned his mouth to hers.

He kissed her, and all his good intentions to
show simple compassion were tossed asunder
at the first touch of his mouth on hers.

He kissed her with all the longing in his body
and heart. He kissed her with the respect and
liking he felt for her. He kissed her for all the
wanting and knowing he could never have her.
He kissed her.

Not as a beginning, as her husband-to-be had,
but as an ending—because her place, her life,
would be here and not with him.

THE HIGHLANDER'S STOLEN TOUCH

Terri Brisbin

First published in Great Britain 2012
by Mills & Boon, an imprint of Harlequin (UK) Limited.
Harlequin (UK) Limited, Eton House, 18-24 Paradise Road,
Richmond, Surrey TW9 1SR

© Theresa S. Brisbin 2012

ISBN: 978 0 263 89268 0

Printed and bound in Spain
by Blackprint CPI, Barcelona

Terri Brisbin is wife to one, mother of three, and dental hygienist to hundreds when not living the life of a glamorous romance author. She was born, raised, and is still living in the southern New Jersey suburbs. Terri's love of history led her to write time-travel romances and historical romances set in Scotland and England.

Readers are invited to visit her website for more information at www.terribrisbin.com, or contact her at PO Box 41, Berlin, NJ 08009-0041, USA.

Previous novels by the same author:

THE DUMONT BRIDE
LOVE AT FIRST STEP
  (short story in *The Christmas Visit*)
THE NORMAN'S BRIDE
THE COUNTESS BRIDE
THE EARL'S SECRET
TAMING THE HIGHLANDER
SURRENDER TO THE HIGHLANDER
POSSESSED BY THE HIGHLANDER
BLAME IT ON THE MISTLETOE
  (short story in *One Candlelit Christmas*)
THE MAID OF LORNE
THE CONQUEROR'S LADY*
THE MERCENARY'S BRIDE*
HIS ENEMY'S DAUGHTER*

and in Mills & Boon® Historical *Undone!* eBooks:

A NIGHT FOR HER PLEASURE*

**The Knights of Brittany*

**And in Mills & Boon
WHAT THE DUCHESS WANTS
(part of *Royal Weddings Through the Ages*)**

This book is dedicated to my editor, Anna Boatman,
for all of her guidance, advice, and gentle prodding
in making this story the lovely romance it is now!
Thanks, Anna.

Prologue

'She has to die.'

Ciara whispered it to her nearest and dearest friend, knowing her secret wish was safe with her. The terrible words branded her as a person of the most horrible kind. Nine years of age and already beyond redemption. She sighed, knowing it was true.

The young woman, the current object of their observation, saw nothing but the man waiting for her at the door to the chapel. She looked neither left nor right, making Ciara hate her even more. The only thing worse was that he gazed back at her with the same intensity. Her own heart hurt then, understanding that she was witnessing love.

'Should we trip her?' Elizabeth whispered

back. Ever her stalwart friend, she would see this through with Ciara.

The puddle of mud to one side of the path was appealing, but Ciara shook her head. From the way Tavis gazed at Saraid, he would look at her the same way even if she was covered in the slime and muck. Ciara's breath caught at the strength and clarity of the feelings between Tavis and his soon-to-be wife. Later, when someone asked her what love was, she would describe it as just that—the expression Ciara could see in Tavis's eyes when he looked at his bride.

'Nay,' she whispered, turning away as tears filled her eyes. 'Leave her be.'

Elizabeth looked from her to the couple, now walking together into the chapel, and sighed. 'What will you do, then?'

Ciara shrugged and did not answer right away. The doors to the chapel remained open and, if she'd cared to watch, she could have seen the whole ceremony as Tavis and Saraid promised to love and cherish each other for life. But she walked away and sought out her favourite thinking place, leaving her friend behind to sigh and watch the wedding she could not.

* * *

Hours later, Ciara realised that there was not much she could do about this—she could not kill Saraid and even wishing her ill made Ciara's stomach hurt. So, after considering her choices for most of the afternoon, Ciara accepted that there was only one thing she could do about this.

She could wait for her chance to love Tavis and to gain his love.

She could wait.

And so she did.

In spite of his marriage, Tavis still welcomed her company and their unusual friendship continued. As she gained in years and in knowledge, she was present many times when Tavis would report to her stepfather, the clan's Peacemaker, after carrying out some task for him. Tavis walked her back to her family's cottage after one such journey and Ciara tried to show what she'd learned only that week.

'Cogito, ergo sum,' she said with confidence. Latin was one of the languages she loved and she was, as her tutor had told her parents, quite proficient in it. She waited for Tavis to react, but he simply laughed and shrugged.

'I do not ken Latin,' Tavis said. 'Unlike you, I have only the *Gàidhlig* and some *Scots*. Oh, and a bit of the *English*.' From his tone, she did not think him insulted by her knowledge or embarrassed by his lack of it.

'I could teach you some of the words,' she offered. 'Or to read.' She was his friend and she wanted to help him however she could. Even now at ten-and-three years, she could at least do that for him.

'There are other ways you should be spending your time, lass,' he said, winking at her as he spoke.

Her mother had been speaking, or rather complaining, to him again. She sighed and looked away. Most likely bemoaning that she did not take her needlework as seriously as she did her study of languages or numbers or… well, not seriously at all.

'I hate needlework,' she said, crossing her arms over her chest and lifting her chin. Surely he would not take her mother's side of it?

'Ah,' he said softly, while taking her hand in his. 'Needlework is a worthy task and a necded skill. Along with numbers, speaking your five languages and reading a few more than that.'

He tugged her hand and they continued their walk towards her home.

'If 'tis such a worthy skill, why do you not learn it?' she asked, irreverently. Shrugging off his hold on her, she waited for his answer.

Oh, aye, she understood the different roles of men and women. But as she was exposed to more and more knowledge and experiences by her father, she doubted she could ever simply return to the constricted life expected of a young woman in her time and place. Did her father know that by allowing her education to surpass other girls her age, he was creating a need within her to learn more and more? Since Tavis was still a man, she waited for his rebuff of her challenge.

'I can already sew, lass. Many warriors have need of it after a battle. Needlework is no different than that,' he answered as they arrived outside her parents' cottage.

Then he offered her the most beautiful, most irritating, aggravating smile, the one that told her he was certain he would be victorious over her in this matter. Ciara wanted to stomp her foot and scream. Of all the things she thought safe to challenge him on, why did it have to be that? While still considering what to say next, he reached over and lifted her chin so he could look at her as he spoke.

'My sister Bradana and Saraid are both skilled at it,' he began. Glancing over his shoulder at her door, he leaned in and whispered, 'And both softer taskmasters than your mother. Though you should never tell her I said such a thing.' He released her and stepped back, motioning towards her home. 'I can speak to either of them about it, if you wish?'

How had this happened? She had manoeuvred herself right into doing the one thing she most wished to avoid. All by trying to show off her skills to her friend. Without uttering a word of surrender, she just nodded and walked away. Ciara almost reached the door when he called out to her.

'I will tell Saraid to expect you on the morrow.'

Ciara did stomp her foot then and slammed the door behind her as she pushed inside, making it rattle the frame on which it was hung. Tavis's laughter echoed outside as he walked away.

As much as she'd like to ignore his offer and refuse to practise sewing and embroidery, Ciara could not. This was another instance of him guiding her to the right choice. She let out an exasperated sigh and walked into her room. Her gaze went right to the collection of wooden animals that sat on her mantel. Tavis had been her friend forever, or at least since she'd been only five years and he came with her stepfather to bring her to Lairig Dubh—her new home and new family.

Though she never wanted to admit he belonged with someone else, watching him with his wife had given her a glimpse at true love. Just as her parents' marriage was a love match, Tavis and Saraid's was as well, even she could see it now. And just as Tavis would do anything to make Saraid happy, so she would do for him—even if it meant becoming proficient with a needle and thread.

Ciara showed up at Saraid's door the next day and on many other days, too. Sometimes she remained after her lessons to help the young woman. Sometimes, may God forgive her weak character, she remained only to see Tavis. Saraid, for her part, seemed to understand that Ciara was important to her husband and accepted her presence and help. Tavis approved and Ciara found herself drawn into friendship with Saraid. With younger siblings, Ciara was familiar with being the oldest sister, but with Saraid, she felt like the younger one, for they were nearer in age than Ciara was to Tavis.

Over the next few years, Ciara grew in her knowledge and skills until her father allowed her to assist him in his work for the laird. But the kinship that developed between her and Tavis's wife was torn apart when Saraid died and a distance grew between Ciara and Tavis, too.

As close as they'd been, nothing Ciara said or did mattered to or helped Tavis in his grief. Some time passed before he seemed at ease with her again, but the recognition that she was growing up and reaching adulthood changed things between them. Tavis began taking on more and more duties and travelled on the laird's business almost as an escape, she thought, from having to face the village alone and to avoid the now-empty cottage where he lived.

Ciara continued to excel in her studies and her father allowed her to accompany him and to read his contracts and documents, leaving her little time for needlework or other womanly skills. And that suited her just fine. By that time, Tavis's attentions were focused solely on his duties to the laird and anything she did went unnoticed by him.

And still she waited.

Chapter One

Lairig Dubh, Scotland—spring, AD 1370

Ciara Robertson sat away from the table, almost in the corner of the room her stepfather had chosen for the meeting. It was a large chamber and comfortable, but did not offer too much comfort. The shuttered windows were open, allowing the cool spring breezes in. Food and drink were offered, but sparingly. This was not about hospitality—this was about business.

She met no one's gaze and most of the men there probably thought she was a servant awaiting their orders. But she was no servant—she was the eldest daughter of the MacLerie peacemaker, Duncan, and was being trained by him even now.

As he had instructed, she listened to every word said, watched the expressions of those speaking and even the way they sat or gestured to gain an understanding of who held the true power in these discussions. 'Twas not always the oldest or wealthiest or the loudest, he'd told her many times. The true power usually sat out of the attention. The true power delegated to lessers and set their leash. The true power spoke quietly and wielded their control carefully.

Now listening and watching, she believed that the MacLaren's younger brother was the one making the decisions in this series of negotiations for a trade agreement with the MacLeries. Though another man, older and calmer, spoke the MacLaren's position, it was clear to her he was not in charge.

The session went on for a few hours, each side clarifying and posturing, and several times Ciara had to force the smile from her lips as she watched her stepfather work—pushing here, cajoling there, complimenting egos, urging that one or the other—to get the best terms for the MacLeries. By the time they agreed to complete the agreement in the morning and break for their evening meal, Duncan the Peacemaker had guided the MacLarens down the paths he wanted them to follow and would close the deal on the morrow. She stood, curtsying to them as they left, and waited for her stepfather to discuss the day's work.

She understood how he worked, for he'd not taken notes during the talks, but he would remember every word and clause agreed to by both parties. He would write down his thoughts and plans before speaking to anyone, so she did act the servant then, pouring ale into cups and giving them to the MacLeries remaining in the room now. Her uncle the laird and the laird's steward waited for her father to collect his thoughts and speak about how to bring these negotiations to a successful conclusion.

A few minutes passed and it felt good to stretch her legs and walk after sitting quietly for such a while. Quiet and sitting were not her usual custom of behaviour. The laird's gaze followed her, but when she met it, he smiled and looked off. Her stepfather, the only father she'd ever known, raised his head and cleared his throat, signalling that he was ready now to discuss the day's progress, or lack of it, with them. He surprised her with his first words.

'Ciara, give me your impressions of the talks

today,' he said. He smiled reassuringly at her and nodded for her to begin.

Words stuck in her throat as she tried to say something useful, something pertinent, now that she'd been asked. While talking in private, giving her opinion or making observations had never been a problem at all. She enjoyed a spirited debate with the man who'd raised her as his own after marrying her mother and she never felt worried over her words. Now though, with the laird and his steward watching and waiting, her palms grew sweaty and her mind went blank.

'Do you think the laird will agree to my request to lengthen the term of this agreement?' he asked, clearly guiding her in her reply. Ciara put the others present out of her thoughts and replied as she would if only speaking to Duncan.

'I think the laird is willing to extend it as you've asked, but I suspect his brother is not. And it is his brother who will make the decision.' What if she were wrong? What if her observations were completely backwards?

Duncan looked at her intently and then glanced at the laird. Connor MacLerie could be intimidating when he wished to be so and, right now, his expression grew dark and his face stern. Had she made an error? She reached up and wiped her hand across her forehead where small beads of perspiration were gathering now, too.

'Did I not tell you, Connor?' her father said to the laird. Had she made a mess of the first time she was permitted to observe? How could she tell her mother, who'd supported her in her education and encouraged her along this unorthodox course for a young woman? If she failed now…

'Aye, Duncan, you did,' the laird replied, now smiling. 'The lass is a bright one and sees through their posturing.' Connor nodded to her. 'And it did not take her as long as it took me to see it.'

Her stepfather beamed, pride in his eyes and a smile on his lips, and Ciara realised she'd been correct.

'What else, lass?' the laird asked. 'Tell me what else you noticed during the discussions.'

'The cattle interested his brother more than it did MacLaren. And I think he is overestimating the men he can call to arms if needed,' she said.

A little more at ease, she explained how she came to her conclusions and answered ques-

tions from the laird, his steward and her stepfather. They discussed the concessions they'd
got already and ones they still wanted.

Only a loud banging on the door had interrupted them some time later.

'They will not serve until you are at table,
Connor,' his wife, Jocelyn, said, glaring at each
of them as though they could have hurried the
laird when he did not wish to be. 'Everyone is
waiting to eat and you dawdle here. Even the
MacLarens sit waiting.'

Ciara tried to hold her laugh in, but the sight
of this powerful man being cowed by his wife
and not resisting her efforts made her chuckle.
Her father flashed a warning frown, but she
could see the mirth in his own eyes at seeing
Jocelyn badgering Connor. Her mother did not
hesitate to speak boldly to her stepfather and
Ciara suspected that she might be waiting to do
just that in the great hall. But, as Jocelyn had
held her tongue until none but family remained
to hear her, so would her mother.

Watching as the laird took his wife by the
hand, entwined their fingers and walked at her
side, Ciara now understood that the laird and
her father did not simply allow their wives be-

haviours that other men might not. They accepted them completely in a manner that could be explained only one way—they loved them.

Having accompanied her father on many journeys on the laird's business, Ciara also understood that it was not the usual custom in most other clans or marriages.

Would she find that in her marriage?

Though not meant to, she'd overheard her parents discussing her marriageable age and about the possibility of seeking a betrothal for her. The time for that was quickly approaching. The dowry bestowed on her would only increase the offers and her ties to two very powerful clans would increase her importance to others who coveted a closer connection to either or both of them. She would be the usual bride—one bartered for her perceived value and not her own worth.

No man would value a woman who was smarter than he or who could understand how legalities worked. Men wanted a woman to fill their bed, oversee their households and lessen their burdens. Whether they knew it or not, her parents had prepared her for a life and for a husband who did not exist. Fortunately or unfortunately, that dowry would plough through most objections right away.

Well, one man would be able to look past all of her accomplishments and see the true woman inside. One man always had and surely he would again.

Tavis MacLerie.

She had kept her true feelings a secret these years from all but her closest friend and confidant Elizabeth, but she'd not forgotten or given up on him and the possibility of something more between them. As a child, she had not realised what that meant other than a fanciful dream, but now she did.

And she was ready for more to happen between them.

The small group walked through the great hall, approached the raised table and she took her place at her parents' side for the meal. The laird introduced her by name to all the MacLarens present and, other than a few raised eyebrows, none expressed surprise at her name. During the talks they most likely thought her only a maidservant to the MacLeries. Now, they understood her standing and things would change.

The glint in the MacLaren brothers' eyes

made it clear—she was something to include in the agreement, a tangible way to strengthen their position with the MacLeries. A brief but telling glance between the brothers made this development clear to both of them and now their demands would change to include a betrothal.

The rest of the meal moved past her in a blur, for she became lost in her own thoughts. If talk of betrothals and marriage contracts would begin in earnest, then she could not lose any more time and chance losing Tavis forever. In spite of his being yet trapped within his own grief of losing his wife, this was now the time to broach their own future.

The negotiations concluded after several more days of discussions during which her name was raised—and squashed immediately by the laird on her behalf. But rather than feeling relief, she knew it had been the first in many that would follow. Soon there would be no rational or legitimate reason to refuse to consider such offers. Ciara knew the time had come and, when Tavis returned from one of the laird's other holdings, she prepared herself to do the boldest, most terrifying thing she'd ever done.

She waited until dark, when she knew he would be alone, before sneaking out of Elizabeth's cottage and making her way to his. Knowing it would be impossible to leave the keep once the gates were closed for the night, she'd made plans with her closest friend, who would cover for her absence, if need be. Now, standing near his door and out of the light cast by the full moon, she raised her shaking hand to knock.

Just tell him how you feel and then ask him, she repeated to herself for the hundredth time since leaving Elizabeth behind. It did not ease her nervousness or increase her courage as she forced her hand into a fist and reached up to tap gently on his door.

You are an educated woman, one who can read and write in five languages and one who can understand contracts and negotiating. You are accomplished in skills and knowledge that most men know nothing of. You are intelligent, quick-witted and any man would be glad to have you as his wife.

The words her stepfather had repeated to

her when her confidence waned echoed in her thoughts, but this time, did not bolster her courage, especially not as Tavis's steps approached her from the other side of the door. She sucked in a breath and tried to calm her racing heart. When he pulled open the door and whispered her name, she lost any hope of it.

He was so beautiful that it took her breath away.

Beautiful was not the correct word, but it seemed to describe his appearance—wholly male, but incredibly beautiful at the same time. Small braids of his dark brown hair hung from his temples and the rest of it hung loose to his shoulders. His tall, muscular form blocked out any light in the hearth behind him as he filled the doorway. Tavis stepped closer to her, glancing behind her and then out on to the path, so close she could feel the heat of his body. Closing her eyes, she allowed herself a moment to enjoy the scent of him, before realising that she must look daft standing before him so.

'Is something wrong, Ciara?' he asked quietly. 'It is late.' She took a deep breath and plunged forwards with her plan.

'I would speak to you, Tavis,' she said, entwining her fingers together to make their shaking less apparent.

'We should speak in the morning…in the keep,' he said, stepping back and depriving her of his scent and his heat. Then a suspicious glint entered his eyes. 'Do your parents know you are walking alone through the village in the dark?'

'I am no bairn, Tavis, and have lived here long enough to know every turn of every path and every soul who abides in Lairig Dubh.'

'So your parents have no idea that you run free.'

Ciara worried her teeth along her bottom lip, not giving him an answer. She did not believe he would turn her away without listening to her first, but the way his face hardened gave her pause that he might do exactly that!

'Best come in out of the chill air,' he said, relenting. He stepped back, opening the door up and waiting for her to enter. Tavis closed the door and walked across the cottage to the hearth. Pointing to a stool nearby, he offered her a seat.

Ciara decided to stand and walked closer to the low fire burning in the hearth. She'd thought about the words she wanted to say for days, but now, standing in his house, the one he'd shared with his wife Saraid, all of them scattered, leaving her silent.

'Ciara?' His voice, low and deep, sent waves of pleasure and anticipation through her, forcing her to gather her thoughts and speak of the matter between them. Rather than mincing words, she sought the candour they always shared and got right to the heart of it.

'I have come to speak to you about the matter of marriage, Tavis,' she blurted out. Then she sat down on the offered stool, since now her legs trembled as much as her hands did. Quite proud of how she'd been so very forthright with him, the frown that furrowed his brow surprised her.

'Marriage? Does someone seek your hand, then?' he asked. 'Does Duncan favour the suit?'

'Nay, no one has offered,' she said. Not as yet, not a serious offer, though with her age and her dowry, 'twas only a matter of time. She wanted to get this settled before they would begin in earnest.

'Do you fear marriage, then?' he asked, concern lacing his tone in spite of his own terrible experience in the marital state. 'Marian would speak candidly to you about that, lass.'

Ciara closed her eyes for a moment, prayed for courage and then said the words that would damn her or give her her heart's desire.

'I would marry you, Tavis.'

The air in the cottage stilled and not a sound could be heard, though Ciara was certain her heart pounding against her chest must be loud. Tavis did not move. His gaze remained on her face, but he gave no sign that he had heard her or, indeed, that he even yet breathed. Moments passed—mayhap hours did, too—while she waited for him to say something to her. Heat flushed in her cheeks and her stomach began to grip. She brushed some loosened hair back away from her face and then repeated her words, for by some chance, he must not have understood them the first time.

'I said I would marry you.'

'Ciara,' he said—her name on his lips was almost a plea. 'Do not—'

'I have much to offer,' she rushed out the words. 'I can read and write in five languages and know how to cipher. I bring a good dowry to the marriage and I...' She stopped then, watching all the colour drain from his face. This was not going well. So she delivered the last bit she was certain would convince him of the rightness of this. 'And I love you, Tavis.'

Whatever reaction she expected of him—surprise, understanding, acceptance—she received something completely different. He startled as though slapped and began to shake his head. 'Do not say such things, lass.'

''Tis the truth, Tavis. I have loved you for years, even before you married Saraid...' She gasped and clamped her hands over her mouth, though too late to avoid mentioning the one name about whom he would never speak.

'You do not know what you are saying, Ciara. Marriage is not possible between us for many reasons,' he said without meeting her gaze now. He turned and faced the hearth, his body tense and his voice hollow. 'I have told you. I will not marry again.'

'But I will be a good wife to you, Tavis,' she pleaded, unable to stop the words now that she'd begun. 'My parents like you and know you and I would not have to leave Lairig Dubh.'

Silence stood between them as she waited for him to see the wisdom in her plan, even if he could not see the love in her heart. Then he faced her and the expression in his eyes was bleaker than she'd ever seen. She shuddered at the profound sadness and knew her cause was lost.

'You have been raised to make some man a wonderful wife, Ciara, but that man is not me. I have nothing to offer you that you do not already have more or better of—I cannot read or write, I have no fortune or blood ties to match yours. Your parents may know me and like me, but the laird intends a marriage for you that will bind clans together. Your fortune is meant to add to your husband's wealth. I am simply a soldier in service to his laird and not high enough in standing to ever gain a bride such as you.'

He shook his head once more at her and her tears rained down. The final blow was about to fall and she could see it coming her way.

'And I cannot love you, lass. My heart was given once and I have nothing to offer you now.'

'But, Tavis…' she began to argue. She had enough love for him that it would be enough. 'I have loved—'

'Stop!' he shouted. 'Do not say such things.' He paced around the cottage, making it feel so much smaller than just moments before. 'You were a child when you decided you loved me and you must grow up now, Ciara. I simply paid heed to a little girl on a journey, befriending her as she grew up. That is all that is between us. You must put aside such childish notions now, for there can be nothing more.'

The pain could not have hurt more if he'd used a real blade instead of his words to strike at her. But that pain made her realise how foolish her words and her actions had been this night. He did not want her. He did not love her.

He would not marry her.

She'd waited for him, waited for his pain over losing Saraid to ease, and waited for him to accept her as an adult, but it was clear he never would. Though foolish, she was not daft, so Ciara used the edge of her cloak to dry her eyes and wipe away the worst of the tears. Humiliated for having so misjudged his feelings and her plan, she stood then and walked to his door. She had to get away from here as quickly as possible. Lifting the latch, she stumbled out into the cooler air, trying to catch her breath, as the tears streamed freely down her face now.

He spoke her name, but she would not, could not, look back at him. Sympathy or pity, she cared not for either right now. Her feet took her down one path and up the hill towards Elizabeth's cottage. She thought he might have followed her, but she never paused and never looked back. When Elizabeth stepped from the shadows to meet her, Ciara felt him stop.

Elizabeth took but one look at her and opened her arms, allowing Ciara to step into them. Though younger by a year, her friend always seemed to be the older one and, for now, Ciara accepted her comfort. When she could breathe again, Ciara stepped back and took Elizabeth's arm, walking beside her the rest of the way. They sneaked back in and soon they were lying in the bed in the loft, though sleep would not come that night.

Only then did Elizabeth dare to ask for details of her talk with Tavis. Though there were many words she wanted to say, none of them mattered any longer. Only one thing did.

'He does not want to marry me.'

Worse, she realised in that moment that the very things her parents had done for her—providing her with a dowry, an exceptional education and making certain her links to two powerful lairds were known—were exactly what now placed her out of reach for Tavis. Had they done that a-purpose? Did they make her so appealing and valuable that only those outside the MacLeries or Robertsons would be eligible for such a bride? Did they wish her gone?

She turned those thoughts over and over in her mind that night and on many others as she tried to recover from this crushing emotional loss.

The next days and months were difficult, but whether by plan or by providence, Tavis seemed to travel on the laird's business more than before and they did not meet face to face for some weeks. By that time, her embarrassment had faded and she could almost believe she'd dreamt the whole encounter. Only a fleeting expression in Tavis's gaze when they spoke the next time convinced her it was all real— far too real.

She spent the time facing the possibility that Tavis had been correct about the nature of her feelings towards him. As eligible men were presented to her, she realised she might have to put aside the dreams of her childhood and face the realities of adulthood.

And when her father announced a possible match one night at supper while Tavis was present and he did not even flinch, she forced herself to accept the facts. She would have to marry a man she could never love.

For in spite of any growing up and regardless of the foolishness of her feelings, she, too, had given her heart away.

Chapter Two

Late summer, AD 1371

The sun broke through the cloud-filled sky,
piercing the greyness and brightening the village
around him. It should have lightened his
spirits, since he liked not the usual autumn
storms, but it did not. Tavis MacLerie crossed
his arms over his chest, set his teeth edge to
edge and shook his head once more to add to
his refusal.

As the laird's man, his job was to assign
warriors to whatever purpose or task that the
laird required, but this time he would not relent.
Many times he accepted the assignment, doing
Connor MacLerie's bidding outside the village

of Lairig Dubh. But not this time. Others would have to see to this…task.

'Explain yourself,' Connor said in a low voice that worried him more than if the laird had shouted his words. Something within Tavis sparked and his muscles gathered as though he'd been threatened and his body was ready to fight.

'I have other responsibilities,' he replied, meeting the stern gaze of his laird without flinching. 'Young Dougal and Iain can see to this journey.'

Connor had recently arranged a tentative marriage contract between Duncan's step-daughter and the heir of an ally clan—the third in a series of never-completed contracts—and all it needed to go forwards was for Ciara to visit the other clan and accept the offer. Her parents were about to leave on the laird's business, so they could not travel with her. Ciara seemed to favour this offer from the Murray clan in the east of Scotland and this trip would be crucial in finalising the arrangements. He'd heard all of this from others, for he'd not spoken directly to her since that night in his cottage.

He could see her face, ashen at his refusal

that night, in his mind. It plagued him even now, but he'd spoken the truth to her that night. He would not, could not, remarry. He had not shared the whole of his reasoning, for it would damn him in her eyes and in the opinion of anyone who knew of it. The fear of someone discovering the full and terrible story of Saraid's death held him apart from the clan and kept him from believing that there could be a happy wedded life in his future. He shook himself free from the memories and the regrets and waited for Connor's answer.

At his refusal, Connor and Duncan exchanged glances that spoke of some kind of message between them. Then Connor nodded his acceptance.

'Tell them to be ready two days' hence,' Connor ordered.

Tavis nodded and turned to leave, relief flowing through him now that he did not face the task of taking Ciara Robertson to meet her betrothed. Startled at that emotion within him when he had denied caring about her in that way, Tavis took no time to dwell on it. As he left the laird's chambers and walked down the stairs to the hall below, he found Marian Robertson, Ciara's mother, waiting for him.

'Tavis, I would speak to you about the journey to Perthshire,' Marian began.

'Marian…' Did she know her daughter had come to his cottage and proposed marriage to him? And that he'd refused her? What could he say?

'Marian!' Duncan's voice called from above them on the stairs. Sharp, but not angry in its tone, the interruption stopped her from saying whatever else she'd planned to say to him. Duncan soon joined them, placing his arm around Marian's shoulders and drawing her near to him. 'Tavis has assigned others to escort Ciara. She will be safely delivered to meet her betrothed.'

Tavis did not like the way those words sounded. He'd known Ciara since she was five and he'd entertained her on the journey back from Marian's family in Dunalastair. Though he tried to think of her as she was now, it blurred with his memories of those days when she'd laughed and played with the wooden animals he'd carved along the way. Now, she would marry and move away and he'd rarely, if ever, see her. His gut tightened at such a thought, though he still did not wish to examine the reasons for that feeling too closely.

He had no right to expect anything more when it came to Ciara. The night he had rejected her he'd relinquished any possible claim to her, if there was one. And he'd humiliated both himself and her in order to force her to accept that they could not be together.

'Duncan, since we cannot go with her, I would feel better knowing that Tavis himself...'

'Do you question his ability to carry out his responsibilities to his laird, Marian?' Duncan released her and took a step away, tilting his head to see her face. 'Surely you do not?'

The hairs on the back of Tavis's neck bristled. Something strange was afoot. He'd never heard Duncan or any of the other MacLerie men ever warn off their wives in such a way. They all accepted the strong, opinionated women they'd married and allowed them much freedom to express their preferences.

This was different, and he was somehow in the middle of it. Without a doubt, he knew he was involved and this was about more than simply assigning men to protect their daughter. He waited for Marian to answer this challenge thrown down by her husband and instead was shocked by her reaction.

'You are correct, husband,' she said. Nodding

to him, she continued, 'I did not mean to question your abilities or your authority, Tavis. Forgive my words, they were spoken in haste.'

He knew his mouth dropped open, but before he could say a word, Duncan took her hand and they excused themselves. He heard them whispering to each other as they walked out the door to the yard and left him standing there, gaping like a fool. Tavis reached up and ran his hands through his hair, trying to sift through the conversation and figure out why it all felt so strange to him. Never a man to leave things unsettled, he followed the couple out, intent on getting an explanation. And he would have done had the very subject of the discussion not been standing there with her parents.

When had she grown up so much? Had he fooled himself into only seeing the girl he'd first met in Dunalastair and, refusing to realise that she'd left that child behind years ago, failed to notice that she had become a stunning young woman? Regardless of his arguments to her that night, he lost his breath as he truly took note of her, and saw, for the first time, the woman she now was.

Taller than her mother and lithe, Ciara wore her long blonde curls loosely gathered into a braid. Unruly it must be, for wisps surrounded her heart-shaped face like a gentle golden cloud. Her gown flowed over curves that spoke of womanly softness in spite of her slender figure. His body reacted in a most unexpected way...

Well, unexpected when he had never thought of her in such a manner before. And unexpected since he'd told her that he had sworn off ever caring for a woman again.

Tavis shook away the memories that were never far from his thoughts and stepped back into the shadows to watch the exchange between Marian, Duncan and Ciara. A myriad of emotions passed over Ciara's face—first interest, then surprise and then bitter disappointment. But when sadness dimmed the brightness of her brown eyes and the smile he usually noticed on her face had slipped away completely, he discovered he'd walked forwards from the shadows, wanting to make that sadness go away. Her stark expression when she noticed him coming towards her forced him to stop before he took another step.

His confusion over his own reaction to her grew as she turned and walked away without another look or word. Tavis continued on and reached Duncan and Marian just as they began to walk away in different directions.

'What is this about?' he asked. Tavis stood blocking their path. He meant to get answers. 'As I told Connor, I have other tasks to see to, Duncan.' Even now his words, the objection, began to ring hollow to him. Did they hear it? His resolve to avoid Ciara began to crack.

'There is nothing to worry over, Tavis,' Duncan said. 'We just told Ciara who you've chosen to take her to Perthshire and she's gone to see to her packing for the journey.'

Ripples traced an icy path down his spine. Duncan did not reveal the truth of what was going on, but surely…

'Marian? Are you at peace with the arrangements then?' She opened her mouth and then shut it, repeating this action several times, each time watching her husband out of the corner of her eyes. 'Have I offended you in some way by assigning the others?'

The flash in her eyes was the only warning either man got before she stamped her foot and shouted. A sound of pure frustration echoed through the yard. Then she closed her eyes, took in a deep breath and released it; all the while Duncan watched her with what Tavis thought might be amusement in his gaze. This was amusing?

'Only that I am disappointed that you will not accompany her,' she began until Duncan cleared his throat, gaining her attention for a moment before she glanced back to Tavis. 'But I understand you have other duties, Tavis. I do understand.'

She touched his arm as she spoke, a gesture he found telling. Her words did not ease the sense that there was more involved than either she or Duncan would reveal, but she did sound earnest in her acceptance.

Ciara was the first of her children to marry and mayhap the emotions of having to part from her daughter was causing this upset? His own mother had reacted strangely when he or one of his siblings married, so it was not unexpected for a woman to behave this way. He nodded his head and she smiled.

''Tis well, Marian,' he said softly.

Duncan nodded, too, and then Marian turned as they all heard her name being called. One of the women who served the laird's wife waved to her and Marian excused herself to go back into the keep and see to Jocelyn's call.

Tavis waited until she entered the stone

building and turned back to Duncan, believing that he would explain everything now that his wife was gone. Instead, the man who he counted as his mentor and his friend shrugged and left him standing there.

This day grew stranger with every passing moment, so Tavis decided to carry out his duties and not worry over this strange behaviour from those not old enough yet to be daft, but old enough not to act so foolishly. In two days, Ciara would leave to meet her potential husband and his family and she would not be his concern at all.

In reality, and although the choice was in her grasp, there was little chance of her not marrying young James Murray. She'd turned down three other proposals, but this time the laird and her parents supported the match. The Murrays supported the match. So, the next time he saw her, she would be marrying someone else.

Though he could not admit it, nor could he explain it, that fact did not sit well with him.

Not at all.

Marian made her way to Jocelyn's solar where her friends had gathered to discuss their plans. Though forbidden from trying to make a better match for her daughter than the one suggested by the laird, due to this stupid agreement with their husbands, she could at least know what her friends were doing. Duncan was not happy with her, for he knew she was about to interfere, and she would have blurted out the truth of it to Tavis if not for her husband's interruptions.

More than a year ago, the laird had discovered his wife's matchmaking scheme and his surprise had turned into a challenge about whether he and his advisers—the men—could choose a better spouse for their children than his wife and her confidantes—the women—could. Neither side worried that the other would not choose carefully, they simply believed they could choose better. Unfortunately for Marian, her precious daughter was the first to come of age and be ready to marry.

Now, as Jocelyn gathered them together to discuss their plan, Marian had to listen and not offer any suggestions or help.

'He did not express any objections to her marrying young Jamie Murray,' she finally blurted out when she could stand it no longer. 'Not a word.'

The silence that met her statement was followed by tsking and sighing, but no one offered any advice on how to make Tavis see the truth that each of the women gathered there had seen for years—he was the best man for Ciara. He'd shunned any attempt to get him to consider marriage again after his young wife died in childbirth four years before. Though men could be stoic and never admit to the softer feelings, they suspected that it had played a part in his resistance to finding another wife since that time.

And through those difficult years since Saraid had passed, the only woman he did keep company with was Ciara. Their friendship had never waned since they'd met on her journey here from her home and clan. Nearing manhood, Tavis never shunned Ciara's attentions or company, even though most young men that age would have. At least not until this last year, when something had clearly happened between them— something that had widened the gap.

'I had such hopes of him acknowledging his feelings for her and saying so by now,' Margriet, Rurik's wife, said.

'He watches her even when he does not realise it,' Jocelyn offered. 'But 'tis time for him to step forward and claim her.'

'Before it is too late,' Marian whispered, knowing that once Ciara left on her journey there would be little or no opportunity to stop the coming marriage.

Or mayhap it was? Or they were wrong in their belief that he was the right match for Ciara? Her heart worried so much for her beloved daughter and for the things Ciara did not, and hopefully would never, know about her true parentage.

Because of those secrets of the past, Ciara's wealth had been inherited from a settlement made by Marian's brother, the laird of the Robertsons. It was a powerful enticement for offers of marriage, as was her connection to the influential Robertsons and to the powerful MacLeries. There had been a number of offers, each met with polite uninterest on her daughter's part.

However, about two months before, Ciara had suddenly accepted the match with young Jamie Murray. Marian knew that something had happened to make her resigned to marry, but no amount of questioning got an explanation. Unwilling to force it from her, Marian accepted her silence on the matter and hoped for the best.

Jocelyn stood then and lifted her cup, waiting for the rest of the women gathered there to do the same. Though she felt little hope that true love would win out in this situation, she raised hers and fought off the tears that threatened.

'To the best husband for our beloved Ciara,' Jocelyn offered.

'To the best!' the others chimed in, touching the rims of their cups and then drinking from them to seal the words.

Marian drank the contents of her cup in one mouthful and shook her head. She did not have a good feeling about this or about Ciara's happiness. 'From your mouth to the Almighty's ears,' she said, offering up a prayer that He would pay attention to a mother's earnest prayer for a beloved daughter.

Chapter Three

Ciara could not stop herself from seeking him
out in the crowd. This feast was in her honour
and she'd hoped against hope that Tavis would
attend, but once more, she was foolish to har-
bour such desires. They'd not spoken since that
humiliating night and she'd not had the courage
to approach him since. Even if she wished to
admit that he'd been right about her infatuation
with him, she could not take the step to tell him
so. Now though, as she prepared to take this
next huge step in her life and begin to move
from this clan to another, she wanted to speak
of it—to remove it from plaguing her thoughts
and her heart as she left the MacLeries.

Elizabeth sat at her side and Ciara smiled
when her friend touched her hand in silent ac-

knowledgement of her sadness. It was a sign of her faithfulness as a friend, even when she knew not the whole truth of the matter.

'You need only tell your parents you do not wish this match to go ahead and they will find a way out of it, Ciara,' she whispered.

'I know that. My parents would not force me into a marriage I did not want, Elizabeth. But Tavis was right when he said I must grow up and seek an appropriate marriage.'

The words sounded calm and very mature, but they burned her tongue with their bitterness. Doing the adult thing and accepting and liking it were two different matters and she feared the second would come much more slowly than the first had. Worse, her parents' efforts to find her a suitable husband had not slowed one bit, despite her efforts to break three betrothals. The feeling that she was being pushed away grew, even though she knew they loved her.

However, a Robertson girl raised by the MacLerie clan was never really part of either family. That fact was hard to ignore.

'This match has much to offer both clans,' she repeated the line she'd used before, this time as much for herself as for Elizabeth.

Elizabeth squeezed her hand and smiled. 'If you are certain, then?'

'I needed only to see that my feelings were just the ones from my days as a bairn,' Ciara explained as she tamped down any reaction to Tavis's entrance into the hall. ''Twas never true love.'

Her heart pounded so hard she was certain Elizabeth and anyone within ten feet of her could hear it, but they did not react to it as she did. Ciara had mastered the skill of forcing her wayward and inexperienced heart to ignore Tavis, but as he caught her gaze and nodded at her, her stomach joined in, revealing how much he did yet affect her, tightening and threatening to expel the few morsels of her dinner that she had eaten.

She could have, and she would have, regained control if he had walked in the opposite direction or if he'd called out to someone across the large room. But when he made his way over to where she sat with Elizabeth and some other young women of the clan, there was no way to do it.

'Elizabeth, Margaret, Ailsa, Lilidh,' he said nodding to each of her kinswomen or friends as he named them. Then he turned his gaze to her. 'Ciara.'

He smiled at her and she did the same. For a moment, he looked on her as he always had, at least, as he had before that humiliating night. Tavis held out his hand to her.

'May I speak with you, Ciara?' She nodded as she stood, willing, though not expecting, this at all. She clutched her hands, trying to calm the trembling that shook them and revealed his effect on her to anyone observing.

'Certainly, Tavis. Have you eaten yet?' she asked.

Ciara always remembered her duties even as she allowed him to lead her away from her friends. He shook his head in reply, so she nodded at the tables that were bursting with foods of all kinds. Ciara pointed to an open place on a bench and they sat. Her chest hurt from the tension in her, her throat and mouth grew dry and she tried to remember how to think.

So much for putting her feelings for him in their proper place.

One of the servants brought over a platter, another brought over a mug of ale and soon Tavis had food and drink enough to feed an army. She watched the dancing while waiting for him to eat before expecting him to speak. They'd shared many meals in the past, but somehow she knew that this one was different. Several people walked by, offering her their best wishes, though none remained long. Finally, Tavis finished eating, took the just-filled cup and turned to her.

'I want to wish you well in this betrothal,' he said, his voice low and deep. 'And I wanted to explain why—'

She shook her head, stopping his words. 'You were right, Tavis,' she admitted while glancing away. Saying the words somehow confirmed it in her own heart. 'My feelings were childish. I have spent the last year regretting what I did.'

He took her hand in his, pulling her gaze back to his, and smiled at her. Her heart pounded from the intensity of his gaze and she swallowed, trying to lessen the tightness in her throat.

'Ciara, it was my fault as well.' The heat of his hand over hers warmed her heart. 'I should have spoken to you before.' He released her and her hand and heart felt the chill at once. 'I should have explained about...things, but I always thought of you as that little lass from

Dunalastair and didn't realise you were growing up so quickly.' He glanced at her and then away at those caught up in the dance. She recognised several of his own siblings there. 'As I have refused to see my own sisters and brothers growing up,' he confessed. He met her gaze again and squeezed her hand. 'And I would not have you leave angry at me.'

The great hall silenced around them and, for a scant second, all she could see or feel or hear was Tavis. Memories of their first meeting, their journey here to Lairig Dubh, the years since and that night a year ago rushed through her mind in that moment. All of it was over and now she would move on, leave this village to marry and live elsewhere. At least they'd had this time to settle things between them.

Time spun out between them, but then the silence receded and the frivolity of the feast seeped back. Tavis startled, tearing his gaze from hers and dropping her hand. Standing then and taking a step away, he forever placed a distance between them. A space that would be filled by another man. A new family in a new place. Even children, if God granted them. But never him and never his. Ciara felt that separation grow inch by inch until the threads that connected them seemed to stretch and eventually snap. She exhaled the breath she didn't realise she held and smiled.

'I would never be angry with you, Tavis. You tried to convince me to see what I did not want to on that night. I was not ready for the truth then.'

Someone called out her name and she turned to see her parents arrive. One of the laird's most trusted men, the man she called father, travelled frequently on clan business. His height meant he towered over others, save for their cousin Rurik, and meant that he could always find her in a crowd. That skill was useful when she was a mischievous child and right now, talking to Tavis in so candid a manner in spite of being promised to another man, it made the same chills run down her spine as any misdeed had. With their hands entwined, her parents moved closer to her and Tavis began to inch away from her.

The occasional scolding aside, Ciara knew their love for her was unconditional—they'd supported her through two previous broken betrothals and she knew they'd do it again if she asked them. Taking in a deep breath and releasing it, she knew then that this betrothal would proceed on to a marriage. She owed them and the MacLerie clan nothing less.

'Ciara! Tavis!' her mother said as they reached the place where she and Tavis stood. 'Are you discussing the final arrangements for the journey?'

Duncan watched him with an unseemly interest as he answered Marian's question. He had made the arrangements, selected the men to lead and guard Ciara and her friend on their journey. In spite of that, he had not discussed any of it with Ciara. Until just a short time ago, he'd not planned on even seeing her before the journey, but something had driven his feet to bring him here. Now, their peace made, Tavis discovered he was more bothered by her ability to move on, and her feelings for him, than he thought. She seemed to be able to move ahead through mistakes and find happiness, while he remained locked in his past with no way to leave it behind him.

He watched as her brown eyes shone with love as she spoke to her parents. 'Twas difficult at times to remember that Duncan was her stepfather, for their bond was as strong as any he'd seen between father and child. Then when she pushed the loose hairs from her braid back over her shoulders, he realised she was nervous. She entangled her fingers together as she spoke, another sign that she was uncomfortable.

Hell!

When had he begun to notice such things about her?

Tavis needed to get away from this, from her, before he did or said something that would make this strained situation even more tense. And he felt the need to prove she was not the only one ready to move on with life.

'The arrangements are made. Young Dougal and Iain are ready,' he reported. 'And Ciara—' he dared a glance at her '—is ready?'

'Aye, I am well packed,' she said, smiling at her mother. The slight twitching at the corners of her mouth meant that it must have been a battle to get packed.

'And your journey, Duncan? When do you and Marian leave?' he asked. Ciara's parents travelled on the laird's business as well. They would all meet back here in a month and the wedding would be held.

Tavis walked aside with Duncan, discussing the true reasons behind the negotiator's trip to Glasgow, but he never took his attention off Ciara. Their last encounter seemed like a distant dream as he watched her speaking to her mother. At ease, graceful, confident, *beautiful*—clearly she'd accepted the betrothal and was content in her coming life. So, why did his gut burn at that realisation? And why was he angered at the thought that she now accepted it? He must be going mad.

Duncan explained many things about his trip and the tasks he would carry out on behalf of the clan and the Earl of Douran, but Tavis heard none of it. As the sounds swirled around him and the memories of things past flowed, he saw only her. As a child travelling with her mother from Dunalastair. As a girl of ten years, telling him stories about all he'd missed while away from Lairig Dubh. As a girl of thirteen who offered her sympathies when Saraid passed. As the young woman who showed up at his door in the dark of night to propose marriage to him.

And now, now as a woman betrothed to another man.

'Tavis? Are you listening?' Duncan's low voice broke into his thoughts and his grasp on his arm shook him from his memories.

'I am, Duncan.' He spoke the words, though not certain they were correct.

He stepped back out of the way now as

some of Ciara's friends approached. Gathering around her, they laughed about some matter before tugging her away, but she pulled free and walked to where he stood. She leaned in close and he smelled the scent of heather in her hair.

'No matter what happens, Tavis, I will never forget how much you've done for me. I am and shall always be your friend.'

The kiss on his cheek surprised him. Words were hard to come by just then and harder to say. He forced them out at a whisper so they remained between them.

'And I am yours, Ciara.'

Tears filled her dark-brown eyes as he spoke and he watched as she tried to blink them away. He would never know what pushed him nearer or what made him wrap her in his arms and hold her close. 'Be well. Be happy,' he whispered as he hugged her for a few moments and then let her go.

He'd barely released her when her friends grabbed her and led her to the open space between the tables. The music began and they formed a circle with Ciara at its centre. Laughing and cheering, they danced—celebrating Ciara's betrothal and, whether they realised it or not, the end of their own child-hoods.

Others joined in—wee ones, mothers, fathers, kin of all ages—for they all shared the joy of this betrothal. Tavis threw off his dark feelings and smiled, clapping to the tune as more and more joined in. Then, when one of the clan held out her hand to him, he let some of his past go for a moment and joined in.

They circled and moved back and forth, each of the couples passing the others in a pattern that continued as long as the music played. The players stopped for a brief pause before begin-ning anew and, to his surprise, another of the women stepped forwards to claim him for the next dance. He laughed as he had not in a long time and, when the dance finished, he danced another and another until the feast was done and everyone began leaving the hall.

For the first time since Saraid's death, he'd stepped into the middle of the clan instead of standing at the side watching. As he turned to say farewell to someone who spoke his name, he noticed that Ciara was gone.

Disappointed in some way he could not name, he drank down the last of his ale and walked through the keep and out to the yard.

Since many of those who lived in the village had attended, the gates were still open to allow them to leave. Waving to several of the men who reported to him, Tavis made his way to the path that led to his cottage.

As he saw the outline of it in the bright light of the growing moon, the same stabbing pain flashed through his heart and soul. He never left a fire burning. He never came home to anyone waiting for him. He was alone as he always was, in spite of this night's revelries when he'd allowed himself to enter back into the life of the clan for a few scant moments.

Tavis moved around the croft out of habit, needing not lamp or fire to guide his way while trying to avoid thinking too deeply on the matter. Soon, he lay on his pallet, thinking about his plans for the next few days, trying to find sleep. Instead thoughts and memories jumbled inside his mind and would not allow him to find his rest. Problems and their solutions continued for hours, but the one he thought most about was her.

Ciara.

Part of him was pleased that she had grown out of her silly notions about marrying him. It was a sign that she was more sensible now than a year ago when she had turned down several marriage offers and had made one of her own. It gladdened his heart to know she was contented in this betrothal.

And yet, as he tossed and turned and found no rest through the night, at the same time, he was not pleased. His male pride was pricked now by her ability to leave him behind, as part of a childhood outgrown. Even knowing such reasoning was irrational, and was exactly what he told her to do, did not help him put it from his mind.

The main reason he'd decided against escorting Ciara to Perthshire was that he did not want to encourage her misplaced feelings towards him, but that seemed not to be an issue now. Giving in to the futility of finding sleep this night, he climbed from the pallet and walked to the window, gazing out at the bright moon there.

Tavis did not remember making a decision over the next few hours, but somehow he had gathered what belongings and supplies he would need, packed and now stood waiting in the yard at sunrise when young Dougal and Iain arrived to lead the travelling party east. Though none of his men questioned this change of plans, he was certain it was noticed by many.

Chapter Four

The morn dawned clear and bright, surely a good omen for her journey and her future. Her clothing had been packed in trunks and placed on the wagon the night before. Any personal items she needed she would carry in her satchel.

The line of wooden animals on the mantel of the hearth in her small chamber stood waiting expectantly. Ciara could not decide whether to take them or not, so she spent several minutes staring them down and trying to make up her mind. They'd been part of her life since she had travelled to Lairig Dubh, each one carved by Tavis in an attempt to entertain her.

The first, a horse, was still her favourite because her father—*stepfather*—had asked him to make it for her. The rest were Tavis's idea and over the days spent on the road, her collection included the horse, the pig, the deer and the sheep. Used by her and shared with her siblings, they were worn smooth now, but no less valued by her. She reached to scoop them up when her mother entered her room.

'Taking them with you on your journey?' she asked as she walked over and adjusted the cloak on Ciara's shoulders. 'You never leave home without them, do you?'

'Should I?' she asked. Part of her wanted to leave them and the other part wanted to bring them. Most likely her childish fears trying to push forwards.

'Darling, they are part of you and your life up to today. Do not be ashamed of them, but do not let your past overshadow your future.'

Her mother smoothed her hair back from her face and pressed a kiss on her forehead. It soothed her as much now as it always did. How would she manage without these special moments? Did she have to give up all of this simply to grow up?

'I think I will take just this one,' she said, with more confidence than she felt. Still, these small objects always brought her comfort when she needed it most. She faced leaving behind everyone and everything she knew and loved and becoming part of another family, belonging to one man. Ciara found a scarf in her trunk, wrapped it around the wooden carving carefully and placed it in the leather bag she would carry.

'Elizabeth waits for you in the yard,' her mother said as she slid her arm around hers and walked at her side. 'Her parents have given permission for her to return with you after the wedding. If you would like?'

Ciara smiled. Of all the news she could receive this morn, this was the best. Her most favourite friend would go with her to her new life, a comforting thought.

'You tease me, Mother,' Ciara replied. 'Only if the laird gave permission for Lilidh to join me would my joy be greater.' Her cousin Lilidh and she had spent many hours and days in each other's company and Lilidh would have been a perfect companion for her. But Lilidh, as the laird's daughter, would be married soon and would not be allowed to stay with Ciara and James in Perthshire.

She would have left, walked out of the chamber that had been hers for so long, but one question continued to bother her. Ciara usually ignored it tugging at her heart, but as this betrothal and wedding came nearer to reality for her, she could no longer keep it in.

'My father...' she said before her confidence faltered. A quick glance at her mother's face stopped her from saying more.

'Duncan is your father, dearling. Always,' her mother whispered. An expression of such desolation entered her mother's eyes that it hurt Ciara to see it there. Gone as quickly as it came, her mother smiled and touched Ciara's cheek. 'We can speak more on this when there is time. But, now, we must hurry and not keep everyone waiting.'

Her mother turned to leave once more, but Ciara was uncertain if she wanted to let this matter remain silent between them. For too many years, the question about who she was and where she fit in plagued her. Though there were mostly moments where she felt treasured and valued for herself, other moments when she thought the efforts to see her so accomplished and so educated just to make it easier to be rid of her also taunted her. Her self-confidence waned in those moments as it did now. Her expression must have revealed it to her mother.

'I beg you, Ciara. Not now,' her mother whispered without facing her, frightening her more than anything else ever had.

She reached over and took her mother's hand, allowing the matter to drop back to its silent place. There would be time for her to press the issue and get the answers she craved so much.

The two of them reached the path and her father joined them, wordlessly following as they walked through the gate and into the yard of the keep. A small crowd gathered there in the quiet, mist-filled dawn, with a wagon and several mounted soldiers who would be her escort. But it was the tall warrior standing near the wagon, issuing orders in low tones, who drew her attention and made her stop so quickly that her father bumped into her. She would have tumbled to the ground had he not grabbed her shoulders and held her until she regained her balance.

'Tavis,' she whispered, not believing her eyes after his prior refusals. 'Tavis.'

'Let me see if aught is wrong,' her father said, stepping around both her and her mother… her mother, who looked as pleased at Tavis's presence as she was.

'Mayhap he has seen to his other responsibilities and is now free to travel to Perthshire?' she mused aloud.

The dark glance shared between her parents intrigued her, but Tavis's reasons for being here interested her more. Following right behind without pause, she stepped out from his shadow and watched Tavis. Men tended not to explain themselves much and this was one of those times—a few words, a few looks and frowns and they were done. Ciara was just as confused as before, but if it meant Tavis would escort her, so much the better.

'I appreciate this, Tavis,' her father said. Holding out his hand, he continued, 'More than I can say.'

More than I can say.

Ciara sighed then, understanding how many problems her previous behaviour had caused for the laird and for her parents.

No clan wanted their heir embarrassed before others and she had done exactly that twice before in turning down offers of marriage. Even if those offers were handled privately, everyone in the Highlands knew that if the MacLerie negotiator visited, business was being discussed. If his unmarried daughter accompanied him, the subject was pretty obvious to all, as it had been twice before.

The Murrays of Perthshire might be destitute, but they were proud with their own powerful connections and they'd refused to consider this betrothal without first gaining assurances that humiliation at the hands of a 'wilful, senseless girl' would not happen. If her parents accompanied her on this visit, a contract would be expected by all their allies and friends... and their enemies. To forestall all that, it was decided that Ciara would travel to visit her distant cousin, James's mother Eleanor. Outside the MacLeries, no one thought this journey was more than that.

Hence the small travelling group and her parents' 'other commitments' elsewhere on the earl's business to anyone who would ask.

And one more reason she treasured her parents, for they could have simply forced her to marry a man of their choosing with little consideration of her own opinions on the matter. But she suspected that something in their past kept them from doing so...and their obvious love for her.

'As do I,' she added. For many reasons as well.

'We should be on the road, then,' Tavis said, glancing up at the ever-brightening sky. 'The weather will not hold and there are miles to cross.' Tavis nodded to the other men, who began to mount up. Then he glanced at her. 'Say your farewells, Ciara.' He walked away to check the wagon, giving her a moment of privacy with her parents.

Tears filled her eyes and she found the words she'd practised all night while tossing restlessly in her bed were stuck in her throat. But words were not necessary now, she knew that, so she just hugged her parents—the mother who supported her every step and every challenge and the stepfather who was the only father she'd ever known.

'This is not truly farewell,' she whispered as she held them close. 'I will return.'

'You will return for a happy wedding day before you leave us for…' Her mother's voice filled with emotion and all she could do was squeeze Ciara's hand.

'Whatever your decision, love, I…' her father began to say.

'I understand, Papa. I have your backing.' A nod and a grunt followed and Ciara knew, too, that, though she was not the flesh of his flesh, she was the daughter of his heart.

Ciara released them and stepped back as she realised that everyone was already on their horses, including Elizabeth. Cora, an older woman who served Lady Jocelyn for a number of years and would serve both her and Elizabeth as a maid, rode in the wagon. Everyone waited without a word, save Tavis, who held the reins of her horse in one hand and held out his other to her. She handed him her satchel and he secured it on the horse before offering her help to mount.

Once that was done, she accepted his help and in a scant moment sat atop the strong horse she'd ridden for nearly a year now. Gathering the reins in her gloved hands, she nodded to her parents and then to Tavis. At his call, the group began to ride out through the gates, with the wagon at their backs. Ciara released a deep breath and touched her boots to the horse's side, riding off to face her future.

Ciara rode as she did everything else in life—with focus and drive. As she sat atop the huge, black horse Tavis would never have chosen for her or ever permitted her to ride, her intense expression bespoke her attention to the road they took out of Lairig Dubh, east through Dunalastair first, then south to Crieff. The last part of the journey would be easier for it would follow the main road into Perth and into the heart of the Murrays' lands. Tavis set an even pace and offered a prayer of thanks when the sun shone and the clouds scattered across a clear sky for the whole of the first day. It would take them several days to reach Dunalastair, going by way of the MacCallum lands where they would visit Jocelyn's family. Then they would follow the old drovers' roads and paths through the glens and valleys south.

Ciara spoke little as they rode, but chatted with everyone when they stopped on their journey. Whether she was seeing to Cora's comfort in the wagon or walking to stretch her legs or speaking in hushed tones to her friend Elizabeth, he passed her often and spoke to her as well. Never did she hesitate or seem ill at ease during their encounters, so Tavis began to accept that she had relegated him to her past and she looked forward to her future. The first days passed pleasantly, with the weather co-operating and the roads smooth.

Then, as they approached MacCallum lands,

Ciara grew excited. He'd not been back here with her since their first trip through on her way to her new home with Duncan and the MacLeries, but he knew she'd travelled many times with her parents and he was certain she'd stopped here on the laird's business. Duncan had sent word ahead so that the MacCallum laird expected them. Ciara and the women would be pleased, he knew, to sleep on real beds this night after several nights in tents on the trail.

They'd not been in MacCallum lands for too long when a group of warriors met them. Leading it was Jocelyn's brother Athdar.

'Tavis!' he called out as he rode closer. 'Is all well?'

Considering all that could go wrong during the journey and that none of it had, he nodded. 'All is well.' Ciara rode up next to him and smiled at Athdar.

'You grow more lovely with each passing day, Ciara,' he said. Tavis watched as a becoming blush crept into Ciara's cheeks. Athdar had a way with women and Tavis had watched as some in Lairig Dubh had fallen for his words and compliments. 'Who would have thought that such a wee lass would grow into such a beautiful woman?'

Tavis fought back the snort that threatened at Athdar's flowery words. Was Ciara taken in by such blathering? He glanced over to see if she did believe it and found Elizabeth more under Athdar's spell than Ciara. Ciara's gaze was filled with scepticism and mirth. Tavis smiled. He should have known her too smart and too confident in her own worth to fall for such.

'Have you nothing better to do than to come and gawk at visitors, Athdar? Surely the laird can find better things for you to do.' Tavis slid down from his horse, laughing at Athdar's now-disgruntled expression. He doubted his friend was insulted or worried over his words, so he held out his hand in greeting.

'Someone has to offer the women soft words, Tavis,' Athdar said as he clasped hands and then shoved him back. They'd been friends for some years now, being of a similar age. 'You never speak unless it's about fighting or your horse!'

Then, things proceeded the way they usually did when the two of them met—with them end-ing up rolling on the ground, each one fighting to gain control over the other. Testing his strength against an equal felt good after the days of slow riding from Lairig Dubh. It took only minutes for Tavis to overcome Athdar, evening their matches. Standing and reaching down a hand to pull him up, Tavis laughed as they both dusted off the dirt from his cloak.

'Are you ready yet?' he asked.

A dark look filled his friend's eyes and then a shake of his head gave his answer. Years before, Athdar had been beaten, badly, in a fight with the laird's friend and commander Rurik Erengislsson and longed to pay him back. Though now, after having observed the heated glances exchanged between his friend and Rurik's daughter Isobel, Tavis wondered if beating the man wasn't the intention after all. A rising wind, ripe with moisture and the promise of a breaking storm, reminded him of his duties and Tavis motioned the group on, allowing them to precede him to the MacCallum's keep.

In a short time the animals had been seen to, the women escorted into the hall to greet the laird and his men released to seek out their own comfort. The MacLeries and MacCallums had been allies for years now and there had been many marriages between the clans already. None were strangers to him, so once his duties were done and he entered the keep, he offered greetings to the laird and found his way to a table near the middle of the large chamber and sat down.

Soon he heard reports about the conditions of the roads ahead and offers from some of the men there to provide additional protection for their group. Tavis talked with many, ate heartily, but drank sparingly. He wanted to get an early start in the morn and did not want to deal with a thick head from too much ale. Still, it was a pleasant evening and he was passing it among friends.

Ciara watched from the high table as several men, and women, joined Tavis where he sat eating. He had, she realised, made the journey a pleasant one so far. Once the surprise of his presence wore off, a very companionable atmosphere fell into place. Since he'd most likely made the arrangements, he needed no one to tell him their path or their supplies. Both tired and not, she finished the savoury meal prepared by the laird's cook and relaxed in her chair. Watching as he spoke and laughed with others, Ciara savoured the moment and realised something important.

He seemed more at ease here than at Lairig Dubh.

'You are staring once more,' Elizabeth warned in a whispered voice. 'Someone will notice.'

Ciara sighed. She could not help herself. Though things between them seemed settled and comfortable once more, they were not truly. Better than they had been for a year, but not back to how it had been between them. Which was probably for the best since she was travelling to meet her future husband and would soon belong to someone else.

'He seems happy,' she replied. 'He even danced with Morag and others at the ceilidh the night before we left.'

'Are you happy about that?' Elizabeth asked, leaning over closer. 'Have you released him from your life now?'

'Of course,' she began. Elizabeth placed her hand on Ciara's arm and squeezed her as though warning her that her friend would know the truth. 'I do not remember seeing him dance in a long, long time,' she admitted the truth in another way. 'It felt good to see that.'

Mayhap she had released him from her heart after all? As though he knew they were speaking about him, he turned his head and met her glance. As he rose and said something to those sitting at the table with him before walking in her direction, Ciara smoothed her hair back and wiped her sweaty palms across her lap. So much for releasing him.

'Ciara. Elizabeth,' he said with a slight bow to them. 'Are you recovered from the travels of the day?'

'Aye, Tavis,' Elizabeth said in a cheerful voice. 'The meal has been quite pleasant.'

'Would you like to walk a bit before retiring?' he asked them both. 'The storms have moved on and the skies have cleared.' They were on their feet before they even spoke and Ciara heard him laugh. Since all three were familiar with the keep and the lands around it, no one needed to lead and they walked in silence until they reached the yard.

As he'd said, the storms were gone and the evening was clear and cool. Though the end of summer grew nigh and autumn would soon arrive, these days were some of the best for travelling with long daylight. She knew where they would walk even before they reached it—it was

one of the places she most remembered from
their first journey here.

Laird MacCallum's pigs!

She began laughing as they approached, both
from the memories and from the expression
on Elizabeth's face when the usual smell grew
too strong to ignore. Her friend began waving
her hand before her face, trying to weaken the
odour, but pigs were pigs and nothing would
help it.

'I am returning to our chamber, Ciara,' she
said, as she stopped and turned away. 'Enjoy
your walk.' A gagging sound echoed behind
her as she strode away.

'I did not think Elizabeth such a delicate
wee thing,' Tavis said to her. 'A few pigs and
she runs?'

Ciara laughed. Though not raised around
them, pigs did not bother her at all. A leftover
sentiment from her childhood when all animals
held a place in her fascination. Especially those
Tavis carved for her. 'A frail lass to be sure.'

They walked to the fence that surrounded
the pen and watched as the animals rooted
for food. Stretching her legs felt good, so she
strode around the large enclosure at a brisk

pace for some minutes before stopping near the gate.

The recent rains muddied up the ground, which seemed to please the pigs. A few piglets did not bother looking for something to eat; they knew exactly where to find it. She stood beside Tavis and watched their antics in silence.

'Have you met James Murray yet?' he asked. Surprised, Ciara nodded.

'We met at Uncle Iain's gathering in the spring. His family was there, as were some others.'

She grimaced. Not a good topic to raise since two other men who she had since turned down were also there.

'Will this time keep?' he asked, turning to face her. The intensity of his gaze reminded her of many discussions between them. She heard the concern in his voice, but now accepted it for what it was—that of a friend.

'I think so,' she said nodding. 'We both like horses. His parents want and need my dowry. All the things on which to base a marriage.' She said it as she struggled to keep all emotions from her face.

He laughed aloud then; it came from the deepest part of him and rumbled all the way out, echoing across the empty yard. Tavis leaned back and let it out, and continued until he rubbed his eyes. 'You were always a forthright lass, Ciara. I'm glad that has not changed in you.'

'I prefer the truth of the matter rather than the sweet words or blurry image. My parents encouraged it, but I suspect that James's parents do not see it as a good thing. If it were not for the dowry, they would never countenance such a match as ours.'

He lifted his hand up as though to touch her cheek, then stopped just before she felt his fingers on her skin. She closed her eyes for just that moment, but forced them open to watch his reaction. Part of her wished against hope that he harboured feelings for her and would speak of them to her before she gave up every last vestige of hope. But, regardless of whether he did or not, she understood her duty and understood that he was not part of her future. Knowing that she belonged to another man, more so with every mile forwards in this journey, Ciara stepped back and smiled at him, relieved to be on better terms with him.

'Dawn will come early, Ciara. You should seek your bed.'

'Until the morning, then,' she said, nodding and turning away from him.

Ciara paused after only a few steps and turned back to him.

'Do you know of James Murray?' she asked.

'I know very little about him. Only what your father has said of him and his family.'

Shrugging and wondering exactly what she'd hoped he'd say, she walked back to the keep where Elizabeth would be waiting for any gossip. For a moment, she wondered why Tavis did not retire, too. Remembering how a number of women, servants and clan, had approached him as he ate, she suspected whenever he did, it would not be alone.

She tried to pass off the burning in her chest as a sign of partaking in too many of the cook's spicy dishes, but the fire of jealousy was hard to ignore.

Chapter Five

⁓⤳⊸⧉⊶⤲⁓

This part of the journey was harder than the rest of it would be. Once they passed through Dunalastair and reached the main road used to bring cattle south to the major cities for the markets, their travel would level out and ease. He knew that, but Tavis also knew that this journey was getting harder by the step for him.

For the first time since Saraid's passing, he'd become aware of the women around him. Nay, not that he had not seen them, but they began now to appeal to him as women did to men. At the ceilidh at Lairig Dubh and then again at the MacCallums' keep and village, he'd crossed some line in his life. For four years he'd looked the other way, but that had not worked for him. The invitations he'd received, the expressions of wanting and desire in the gazes of several of the women in both keeps, made it clear that he did not have to sleep alone.

That was the usual way of things—a widow's bed could be a welcoming place for an unmarried man in the clan. Nights of pleasures shared without the commitment of marriage vows or until the two were certain they wanted to marry. Or not.

Not that he would ever marry again, but…

The remorse that always filled him whenever he thought of Saraid—her life, their life, or her death—flooded him now and reminded him of the terrible failure that would always be his burden. Bile spilled into his mouth as did the bitterness of his actions when Saraid needed him most. He spat on to the ground but, real or only memory, he could still taste it.

Guiding his horse down the steep pathway that led into Dunalastair's village, he reconciled himself to his fate. But when Ciara raced by him, laughing and calling out a challenge, he put away the dark memories and darker possibilities of his future and followed her.

'To the bridge!' she yelled, tearing off her head covering and letting the wind catch the length of her hair.

Damn, but she could ride! And with the mount she had, he would be hard pressed to catch her now. Tavis spurred his horse on to follow, trying to work out if there was enough distance in which he could catch her before they reached the bridge. Doubtful. Still, he bent low over his horse's neck and urged it on faster and faster.

The wind in his face and the feel of the horse's strong muscles as it pushed them faster along the road forced all melancholy from him. He focused his thoughts on the woman ahead of him, though now just barely. Dirt flew under the horse's hooves and branches whipped him. None of that slowed him down, not when victory could be his. They approached a split in the road and he took the one Ciara did not.

Tavis laughed aloud then, knowing now that he would reach the bridge first by using this path. He'd done it many times when travelling here with Duncan. When he broke through the last of the trees, Ciara sat on the bridge, smiling at him. How had she…?

'You are not the only one who knows the shorter pathways around here, Tavis,' she scolded.

He should have known better. He should

have realised that she would be a fierce competitor even on the way to becoming a dutiful wife. James Murray would not appreciate a woman like Ciara. He was too young and in the power of his parents who, as she'd said, only wanted the match for the money she brought them.

He tipped his head at her and jumped down from his horse. Gathering the reins, he walked to the bridge and held hers while she climbed down. Both of them were out of breath as they entered the village of Dunalastair, walking the horses to cool them down. Ciara had moved from here when she had only five years, so her memories of the place were more from her visits back. Without asking and out of habit, they walked down the lane that led to her mother's old cottage.

'Will the others be offended that I keep leaving them?' she asked as they turned on to a smaller path and stopped before a small cottage.

As he watched, she walked to the edge of the enclosed garden and peeked within. Her mother had a talent with growing herbs and much more and this was where her skills had developed. With Ciara at her side. The tears that glistened in her eyes were no surprise to him. Tavis allowed her some private moments before calling out to her.

'Word will get to your uncle before you do, Ciara. We should go.'

She fumbled for a small pouch tied on her belt, one he had not noticed before, and she ran her hand over its surface, feeling whatever was inside it. Almost as a bairn rubs a blanket when troubled, she repeated the action again. Then her hand dropped and she faced him. 'Aye. Uncle Iain likes to be the first to know when he has visitors.'

'Are your other uncles expected?'

He knew that Ciara's mother had four brothers, two older and two younger, for he'd met them all several times. Padraig, married to a MacKendimen lass, served as Iain's second-in-command and oversaw all Robertson warriors. Caelan, recently betrothed to the MacLean's daughter, oversaw the clan's holdings. Only Graem, now ordained and appointed as secretary to the Bishop of Dunkeld, lived elsewhere and visited infrequently.

'He did not say. This is only a short visit, so I suspect not,' she said as they made their way to the keep on the hill.

* * *

By the time they arrived at the gates, the rest of their escorts and companions caught up with them and they entered together. The men laughed when she told them all she'd won and Tavis knew he would be taunted unmercifully about that when she was not there. He greeted several of the Robertsons as they were guided into the main hall. As Ciara said, this was not a formal visit by the heads of their allies, so few were there to greet them, the rest carrying on their duties.

'Ciara!' Lord Iain's loud voice filled the hall as he called out to his niece.

Tavis watched as she ran to him and was wrapped in his embrace. The older man had never married and had no children, but this niece was special to him. Remembering the rumours and speculation that surrounded Marian's fall from grace when she was known as the Robertson Harlot, Tavis wondered if Lord Iain knew the truth about Ciara's father.

For Ciara did not.

He followed Ciara forwards and waited for her to introduce both Elizabeth and Cora to her uncle before speaking or offering greetings. Reaching inside his leather jacket, he removed the folded parchment he carried to the Robertson laird.

Watching the two speak in hushed tones, he thought they looked more like father and daughter than uncle and niece. He shook his head, pushing all the conjecture away, for if there was an unknown truth between them, Tavis was not and never would be privy to such matters.

And it mattered naught.

His duty was to see Ciara safely to her betrothed and bring them back to Lairig Dubh for a wedding. And he would do that. Then, he would return to his life and continue to serve the Clan MacLerie and the earl. He did not fool himself that he counted as family or stood higher than others who served. As he'd told Ciara that night, she was too high for the likes of him. Now, seeing her being greeted as family by this powerful laird, that fact was pushed in his face and unavoidable. Lord Iain released her, though he kept Ciara at his side, and waved Tavis forwards. He bowed, offering the letter from Duncan.

'My lord,' he said, as he stepped back.

'Tavis,' the Robertson said, reaching out his hand in greeting. 'Welcome back to

Dunalastair. My thanks for seeing Ciara safely on her journey.'

The laird invited them all to supper and directed his servants to see to their comfort. The men divided up, he and young Dougal and Iain would share a chamber off the hall while the others would sleep with the laird's men below. Although he was offered a bath several times by several obviously accommodating maidservants, Tavis decided to use the stream not far from the keep in the woods instead.

It was as he was leaving the keep that the laird called to him for a word. He waved the others to go on and followed the laird to the private chamber off the hall. Offered first a cup of ale and then a seat, Tavis waited to discover the purpose of this meeting.

'So, Tavis, what does she know? What does she remember?'

He was so surprised by the questions he swallowed a mouthful of ale too quickly and choked on it. It took several deep coughs to clear his throat to breathe. And a few more minutes to consider how to answer such questions. Tavis decided on candour.

'She was too young to know or remember any of it. Though the rumours and gossip spread, Ciara would never have heard of it.'

'And the MacLeries?' Lord Iain probed while watching him closely over the rim of his goblet.

'She is as our own. If her mother is still called by anything other than Marian Robertson, it is not done by the clan MacLerie.'

Tavis remembered the night they arrived in Lairig Dubh and how Connor and Duncan had proclaimed her one of them. And they'd made it clear that insulting her was insulting all of them. No one had ever spoken that name again.

If Ciara ever wondered about her father, she had never voiced such a thing to him. But then their talks had focused on horses, animals, horses, his siblings, horses and...horses. Even as she grew, she remained fascinated with them. It was the reason why he'd carved several of them for her over the years since she'd become part of their clan.

Strange—he'd not noticed her lack of interest in her father's identity through all the years he'd known her. By the time she might have been old enough to be curious about a father before Duncan, his own interests and life lay elsewhere.

'And she's never asked you for the truth?' The laird's voice was quiet, but threatening in some way at the same time, as though he suspected more between them than existed.

'Why would she do that, my lord?' he asked.

'Your friendship is known by many.' Ciara's uncle met his gaze and let the words imply what they would.

It took him no time at all to answer the insult. Tavis lifted his fist and swung at the man. The laird side-stepped it easily, giving time for Tavis to realise the importance and foolishness of his action. He dropped his hands to his sides and waited for the laird's response.

When the Robertson turned away and refilled his cup, Tavis shook his head. He had not done something so stupid in a long time. The laird was within his rights to demand punishment for such an offence. Worse, by swinging his fists at him, Tavis had almost confirmed his suspicion that something more existed between him and Ciara than did.

'My lord, I...' He really couldn't finish because he wasn't certain for the first time what to say.

'She told me of her plans to marry you.'

Of all the things the laird could have said,

that was not any of the possibilities he'd thought of. Ordering his imprisonment for one; calling his men to beat him senseless for another; gelding him to prevent any more untoward actions towards his niece—but this? Tavis let out his breath before replying.

'The words of a child, no more, my lord.'

'That is what I have always believed, Tavis. I want to protect her just as you do.' He emptied his goblet and left it on the table where the pitcher of ale sat. 'It is important that no questions be raised about Ciara's virtue during these negotiations.'

'You insult my honour and hers once more, my lord.' Tavis crossed his arms over his chest.

'Nay, I but bring to your attention that others have noticed the closeness between you and my niece. Within your lands, the MacLerie might control what is said, but you left those lands days ago and now expose Ciara to gossip. Gossip that could tie her to a past best forgotten.'

Tavis finished his ale. The laird was correct. Friendship between a man and woman who were not related by blood or marriage was not the customary thing. So, it was natural that others would question it.

'I will see that there is no more gossip, my lord.'

'And I will keep you no longer from your duties,' the laird said, dismissing him. 'Supper is in two hours. It will be ready for you in your chamber.' Tavis turned to leave, but the laird was not quite finished. 'I've decided that two of my men will join you for the rest of the journey south.'

'That will defeat the entire purpose of sending her with only a small escort of MacLeries, my lord,' he began through gritted teeth. 'If the Robertsons join in, then this will look like more than it should be—a cousin visiting a cousin.'

The Robertson stared at him through narrowed eyes and then nodded. 'A wise observation, Tavis. I will leave you to it then.'

Tavis followed him out and continued on his way to the stream. The words and the warning given him weighed heavily in his thoughts. And he considered the other questions asked of him. Had others raised questions about Ciara's father? As far as he knew, no one had been named such and no one had claimed to be him. But, with Marian's reputation and the stories that were yet remembered by many, how would she know?

He took a narrow path next to the keep's gate and followed it for almost a mile to the stream. Young Dougal and Iain already swam in the cool water and he joined them, leaving his clothing in a small clearing by its side. Though they'd ridden through storms and rain, nothing felt so good as this. He dived under and came up on the other bank.

Tavis spoke to the others about the plans for the rest of the journey. They should make good time because the roads ahead were well used and would lead down from the more mountainous lands to the flatter ones as they approached the southern part of Scotland. He had no doubt that Murray warriors would await them near Perth to escort them to the family's keep.

The journey back? He had no idea of what would be involved or who would make it, so he did not waste time worrying over it. After enjoying the refreshing water, they headed back to the keep for supper and a good night's rest.

Iain Robertson returned to his chambers after watching Tavis leave to seek out his men. Pouring a full cup of ale, he sat in his chair and drank most of it in one mouthful.

Watching the grave errors of his youth

brought full circle to him was not easy. He'd had years to wonder how she would turn out and now he could see it for himself—Ciara was a beautiful, accomplished, intelligent young woman that any man would be proud to call daughter.

As he would if he were free to speak the truth. But he could not, for others had paid with their lives and their souls to keep her true parentage a secret.

There was no way now to right the wrongs he'd done in the past. There was no way now to keep the secrets that lay silent with the dead. And when loved ones were threatened, there was no way that oaths sworn under pressure would remain intact.

Iain drank the rest and thought about how much Ciara resembled her mother. Both blonde, both with the same shade of brown eyes. Pushing away the past, Iain threw his cup down and rubbed his eyes and face.

Too much depended on his sister and her peacemaker husband and too many years of not worrying about the consequences now caught up with him. The truth they'd all hidden had kept his clan and their honour intact for these last ten or so years. Was he strong enough now to weather any challenges made if the truth were outed?

God help him, he hoped so.

Ciara feared her cheeks would never stop blushing. Touching them, she felt the heat of it and knew she must look feverish. Elizabeth's had the same red glow, but she was more distraught over it than Ciara was. In the chamber assigned to them by her uncle, she'd sent Cora on some errands so that she and Elizabeth could speak on what had happened. But no words would come.

She had never considered herself sheltered or easily embarrassed or ignorant until now. After organising her clothing in their chamber, she and Elizabeth had decided to take a walk before supper. 'Twas something they did often, especially on this journey and especially after riding so many hours each day.

One of her favourite places on a hot summer's day was the stream that ran along the edge of her uncle's village and the falls that the stream had carved in the hillside over the centuries of running over it. The most wonderful little pool caught the water and she loved to put her legs in the water on hot afternoons when she visited Dunalastair.

They'd sped along the path and reached the stream, intending to turn south along its run to reach the pool. The sound of splashing and men's voices, familiar ones, captured their attention and she led Elizabeth along the banks to find them.

And find them they did!

Though Ciara had seen naked men before, seeing Tavis naked was something she'd dreamt about, but never thought possible. He sat near the opposite bank, in the water up to his waist, his broad chest and muscular arms glistening in the sun that managed to peek through the trees. He dunked his head under the water and shook it back away from his face, giving her a view of his strong back.

When he swam across and climbed out of the water, she thought her heart had stopped! Elizabeth clutched her chest, so she must be having the same reaction. Then her friend covered her eyes and turned away. Ciara allowed herself several additional moments to watch him dress, holding her breath for fear of giving her position away and for fear of making a sound.

A proper young lady would have screamed in fear and shock and run away at first glance. A proper young lady would have covered her eyes or had the decency to faint. She did none of that, instead watching every move he made and never turning away from his magnificently masculine form.

Until Elizabeth grabbed her by the hand and dragged her away.

They stumbled through the trees, back to the path and ran to the falls and the small pool there before stopping. There they'd fallen to their knees, laughing as they did when they did something naughty as girls. Though seeing Tavis naked made her feel something she'd not felt before—an ache that throbbed deep within her and sent tendrils of heat throughout her body. Her mouth grew dry, but she craved... something.

Now, back in their chamber, Ciara wanted to speak of it to Elizabeth, but the image of his body as he climbed out of the water interfered with her attempts to do that. And that led her to thoughts of what being his wife might involve. And *that* kept her blushing at the truth of it as she understood it and unable to speak to Elizabeth.

So, when the call came for supper, Ciara fought to keep all of her confusion and embarrassment inside. Mayhap if she did not look at him, she could control these strange feelings? Mayhap she should beg off and remain here until morning? Once they were on the road, she could avoid Tavis easily until the unease wore off.

Nay, she was a grown woman now and she would soon learn a man's body intimately. Not Tavis's. She would need to put Tavis from her mind. Accepting that she must move on, Ciara rose and walked to the door. As she lifted the latch, she faced Elizabeth and smiled.

'I was wrong today,' she admitted. 'I should not have remained there.'

'He is.. beautiful,' Elizabeth said.

'He is not mine to gaze on that way.'

Her wayward thoughts then brought James Murray into her mind. He was at least a half-score of years younger than Tavis and did not have the training and experience as a warrior that he had either. Though quite attractive, he did not have the wildly handsome features that Tavis did, with his green eyes matching the tones of the forest around Lairig Dubh and his chiselled chin and wonderful mou—

What was she doing? She seemed more under the spell of her childhood feelings about Tavis now than she had a year ago! She met Elizabeth's gaze and could see her deciding whether or not to pursue this. Her friend smiled and nodded.

'I am sure that James will be as pleasing as what we saw today.'

Knowing the truth, they laughed for a moment, until Cora opened the door, urging them on to supper. Ciara had only a few more days, a week at most, to tame these errant thoughts and reactions before arriving in Perthshire. Taking in and releasing a deep breath, she calmed herself and nodded to Cora.

Chapter Six

By the time they reached the hall and walked to the front table where her uncles waited, Ciara believed she had this yearning for Tavis under her control. She greeted her family and cousins and sat down, only then looking around the large room for the rest of the travellers from Lairig Dubh.

'Your MacLeric escorts sent along their regrets. They have other duties to see to so that you can leave in the morn,' Uncle Iain said.

If she had looked away just then, she would have missed it. A slight narrowing in his gaze. A minor lift in the corner of his mouth. All signs to anyone who knew Iain Robertson that there was more going on here than he would admit and that he had a hand in it somehow.

Did he know what had happened at the stream? Did he suspect something between them? Well, no matter. Ciara nodded and placed her napkin on her lap as the servants began placing platters on the table.

'They are ever attentive to their duties, Uncle. Especially Tavis.' His left eyebrow lifted ever so slightly, confirming that he'd ordered Tavis away from this meal.

Ciara would think about this later, for now she enjoyed the meal with her uncles. Since their path back to Lairig Dubh would go in a different direction, she might not see them for a long time. Though they supported this match, the wedding would be accomplished back at her home and she doubted any of them would attend.

Strange. Their affection for her was obvious, yet she did not remember them ever speaking of it outside their lands.

And, thinking about it in the silence of eating, she wondered if it had to do with her father. Oh, no, not Duncan, her stepfather, but the man who had never been mentioned by name to her. Ciara had feared asking about it as it was made clear to her that it was a subject not to be spoken of.

Had her father dishonoured her mother and not married her then? Had he been an enemy of the Robertsons and one not eligible to marry the only daughter of the powerful Robertson laird? Had he died before her birth? She sighed then, wishing she knew the answers to these questions and wondering why she had not the courage to ask them.

The meal ended and she and Elizabeth excused themselves to return to their chambers. Cora was off seeing to cleaning some of her garments, or at least giving them a good brushing to remove the dust of the road.

As she lay in bed, trying to find sleep, all the same questions plagued her. Tossing and turning so much that she disturbed her friend who could sleep through most everything, Ciara climbed from the bed and walked to the one small window on the wall. Pushing the shutters open, she leaned against it and peered into the darkness outside.

Those in the keep were settled for the night. A cluster of nightjars sang their song out of tune and the trees seemed to move in time with it, much as she would dance to music at a ceilidh. Night-time was magical to her and, if she were home, she and Elizabeth thought nothing of walking through the village, talking and sorting out their concerns and making plans.

Why did things seem to make sense in the dark of the night and then not when day's light shone on them?

Unable to figure that out, Ciara climbed back into the bed and finally allowed sleep to claim her.

The rain suited his mood and kept chatter to a minimum as they left Dunalastair behind and joined up with the old drovers' path that would take them to the market town of Crieff. All three women rode, cramped, he was certain, in the shelter of the wagon. He and the other men were not bothered by the weather. He'd lived, slept, ate, fought and...did most everything outside at one time or another. As long as the roads did not turn to mud and the wagon kept moving, they travelled.

Wrapped in the lengths of tightly woven plaid that kept most weather and water at bay, he and the men continued on. The first two days were wet, but the roads passable. On the third day of solid rain, it was as though the fates heard his thoughts; the wagon got mired down and came to an abrupt stop. He heard the startled cries from within and rode back to see if anyone was hurt. Other than a few muffled curses as he drew near, and he knew whose voice they were muttered in, everyone was safe.

'Are we stuck?' Ciara asked, lifting the canvas tarp that formed their canopy out of the way and peering through the downpour at him.

'Aye, you are that.' Tavis jumped from his horse and tested the wagon, pushing against one side. Soon a couple of the men were with him, but no amount of strength seemed to loosen its wheels from the quagmire that trapped them.

'Here, Tavis,' Ciara said as she stood up and tried to get out of the wagon. 'Take my hand.'

'Ciara, wait a wee while until we figure out if this can be freed,' he ordered back.

She jumped, damn her, and landed just next to him, her leather boots sinking into the mud. Without hesitating, she gathered her skirts from behind, pulled them between her legs and secured them to her belt.

'Ciara,' he began.

'Elizabeth, come out now,' she called in to her friend. 'You will not melt in the rain and we need all the help we can get.'

Was she daft? Did she think he was going to let her...?

'If we all help, we can empty the wagon, move it through these rough patches to flatter ground and be on our way,' she said, urging the other girl out from the protection of the covered wagon and into the torrents of rain.

Damn! Did she have to be so sensible? Should she not be sitting inside the cart, moaning and fretting, much like Cora was at this moment, waiting for him and the other men to do what was needed to free the wagon and get them moving again? Instead, with a lack of fear and with a good instinct about how to handle this situation, she took control and gave orders. Within minutes, the other women had secured the long skirts of their gowns as she had and were carrying some of the lighter supplies off to a clearing under the trees.

Tavis wanted to argue with her, overrule her, but she did exactly what he would have recommended be done and got less resistance from her women than any man would have.

It took about two hours to complete, but the wagon was emptied, contents moved and the wheels freed from the mud and moved forwards to a smoother part of the path. Through it all, not one of the women had complained. Later, when they'd repacked the wagon, found a place to rest for the night and everyone was settling down, he realised what bothered him so.

He truly liked Ciara. He liked the woman she'd become. In spite of his declarations to the opposite, he felt more for her than he could ignore. More than would do either of them any good. What he felt and what he wanted did not matter, for she was above him in status and wealth and everything that was important. He had neither the heart nor soul left to offer her marriage and that was the only thing a woman of her class could accept.

Worse, she was promised to another and any interference in the arrangements, secret at this time or not, would still result in dishonour and possibly a feud between the MacLerie and the Murrays.

The Robertson laird must have seen signs of this when he issued his warning. If that man could see it, then others could and would. So, Tavis decided he must look at her and the rest of this journey as he would any other task assigned to him by Connor. Just that—a task assigned by his laird.

He stared across the clearing, from where he stood to where she sat, stirring a pot of simple stew over the fire. As she did so many times before, Ciara lifted her head and met his gaze. Within the depths of those warm, brown eyes he saw everything he felt reflected back at him: confusion, desire, need, wanting and love. Tavis turned away.

They could not. They would not.

Despair, ruin and unhappiness lay ahead of them if they followed their desires. For him it would mean the loss of his honour, for he'd sworn allegiance and obedience to the laird. Worse, for her it would be the loss of everyone she held dear. She would face shame unlike any embarrassment she'd suffered before. They would both be exiled from clan and kith and kin with little hope of sharing even that dishonourable life.

And that was something she would never survive either.

Tavis drank down the ale in his cup and stood. His stomach rolled and he wanted no food now. How cruel the fates were to allow them both to see the truth of something between them just when they were reconciled to the impossibility of it.

As he strode off to check with the two men set as guards, he accepted that the only good thing was that both of them would do their duty and hold fast to their honour.

Ciara thought she knew how her old doll felt the day that she and her younger brother fought over it—twisted, torn and all the stuffing pulled out. As she scooped up the stew and served it to the others, she was certain of what had just passed between them. He'd allowed her to see into his heart and soul and to learn that she was not the only one confused, yet thrilled by the feelings there. Then, as though he'd made a mistake, he left, not even taking the time to eat with them.

This must be the worst part of growing up and accepting your role as an adult with duties and responsibilities to others. And she hated it even at the same moment that she savoured the brief but honest moment between them. For in that instant after he'd turned away, Ciara had thought of all the possibilities and all the impossibilities as well and none of them were acceptable to her. To them.

So, she, they, would follow the path they'd chosen, be honourable and true to their families' expectations. Mayhap the shock of knowing he'd treated her as an adult and accepted what was honest and true in her heart had also caused her to accept the futility of it all?

After cleaning up from their meal, with Elizabeth's and Cora's help, she climbed inside the wagon, under the blankets spread for her use and found that her mind was quiet for the first time in so very long. A certainty filled her now—the unavoidable reality she had never wanted to consider but that now was hers.

She would not marry the man she had loved her whole life.

Four days later, after the night of reckoning as she thought of it, they reached Crieff. Tavis had sent men ahead to find them a place to stay and to make arrangements for the final part of the journey. If any in the group noticed a change between them, none mentioned it. Instead, it was as though Ciara had taken all of her feelings, wrapped them in a bundle and put them aside. Easier to ignore all of it than to have it task her mind, heart and soul during every waking hour.

And sleeping hours, too, for she saw him in her dreams. Except there, he left the stream,

walked to her and kissed her with such abandonment that she woke more than once expecting to find him entangled in her blankets next
to her. Some primitive urge had been awakened
within her and would not cease its demand for
satisfaction.

Crieff was a welcome distraction for all of
them, it seemed. A busy market town, filled
with all sorts of merchants and goods, it was
the first large town they'd seen on their travels. Tavis had sent men ahead to locate suitable
lodgings for the women.

As they entered from the north-west, she
heard Cora and Elizabeth laugh at the sight of
so many people and animals and stalls. She'd
chosen to ride her horse and followed Tavis's
order to stay next to him at all times. With so
many things to look at, it was difficult not to
get diverted, but Tavis soon led them to a qui-
eter street when the buildings were spread out
from each other. They stopped before an inn
and Tavis helped her, then the others, down.
Young Dougal guided the wagon around the
wooden inn to the yard where they would se-
cure it for the night.

Though she probably looked like a peasant,
Tavis made certain that the MacLerie name

and title eased the way to the best room for them. He stayed with them while they found their chamber and waited for Iain to bring in the satchels they prepared for this stay. A bath was promised and Ciara imagined how good it would feel to soak in a tub of steaming water as they climbed the stairs to the upper level that held but two small bedchambers.

'One is for you and Elizabeth, the other for Cora and our trunks,' Tavis explained as the other men began to carry their supplies past them. 'And the innkeeper will set up the bath in here.' Once they were done, Ciara gained Tavis's attention.

'Can we walk around a bit after getting settled here? There were so many interesting things to see,' she asked.

'Did you see the stalls as we passed?' Elizabeth asked. 'It would be such a treat to visit them.'

She and Elizabeth named several more places and people who'd caught their eye as they rode in and Tavis just watched in silence, turning back and forth between them as they spoke. Then he held his hand up, stopping them. Though she had travelled with her parents to cities like Glasgow and Edinburgh,

Elizabeth had not. This trip was a treat for her and Ciara wanted her friend to enjoy all that she could.

'Aye,' Tavis finally said. 'Since it is not yet overwhelmed for the Michaelmas tryst, it is safe enough to walk. Finish seeing to your comfort and I will tell the men.'

Their excitement even spread to the usually calm Cora, who had a few coins with her to buy something that appealed to her. Elizabeth and Ciara both had small purses, too, and permission to buy what they needed or wanted, so it should be an enjoyable few hours.

And it was. The three men who walked with them had joined in the enthusiasm and made suggestions for purchases. It was a surprise to Ciara for she worried that they would keep to themselves as Tavis had done these last days. They arrived back at the inn just as supper was served. The lively conversation and good, hot, well-flavoured food all lent itself to a pleasant evening among people she'd known almost all of her life.

A fitting way to end her life with the MacLeries before beginning one with the Murrays.

Was she destined to be passed from one family to another? Was she wanting in some way that no clan wanted to keep her? She remembered little of her time with her mother's family. The last half-score of years with the MacLeries were all she knew. But most of that time was grooming her to make her appealing to some other clan. Never was a marriage discussed or offered that would allow her to remain in Lairig Dubh—the only place she knew as home.

Trying to push away the maudlin feelings that threatened to overwhelm her, she looked around and noticed that most of all the other inhabitants at the inn had gone off to their rest, so Ciara and Elizabeth sought theirs. The steaming bath, scented with oil Cora had packed away, eased the aches and pains in her body, but not the one in her heart. Tears tracked down her cheeks to blend into the water around her. Silent tears for the loss. Tears for what could never be.

Worse, she now realised that Tavis had been correct—she had played at loving him all those years. Childish worship, all of it. Now, now when she'd thought she'd moved on and was ready to accept that he did not share her feelings, he did.

'Damn him!' she whispered, hitting the water with clenched fists and sending some in a cascade over the edge. 'Damn him.'

And damn her foolish, now grown-up heart.

Chapter Seven

The road leading into Perth from Crieff grew crowded and Tavis kept their small party together as they moved along the way. A royal burgh, Perth was the centre for trade with many other countries across the sea on the Continent. Due to the establishment of so many religious orders in towns nearby, Perth drew pilgrims as well.

The English King Edward had captured it. Robert the Bruce took it back. This left Perth with the strongest stone defences in Scotland now, which were visible as they moved ever closer. A high wall with many towers surrounded it now and they would pass through one of the gates soon. Tavis planned to stop for a meal there before continuing through and to the south-east to reach the Murrays' lands.

Although connected by past generations of marriages and purchase and kinship to the ancient Highland *mormaers of Moireabh and of Atholl,* the lowland branch of the family that Ciara was marrying into was distant in location, wealth and power. Connor believed this match would be good for the clan MacLerie in order to gain access to the important ports of Perth and Dundee, so that was all that truly mattered.

With the weather co-operating, they should reach their destination by mid-day. Ciara and Elizabeth's excitement as they travelled through the city forced a smile from him more times than he would like to admit. They would be able to visit here often once Ciara married the Murray heir.

At least it would be easier than seeing her day in and out in Lairig Dubh. Calling on his honour and hers, seeing the dark abyss of possibilities opening before them and then stepping back from that edge had a sobering effect for him. It made it easier to let her go.

He would have to remind himself of that every day and night from now on. For now, he would see her safely on. He'd sent young Dougal ahead to the Murrays to tell of their arrival. Once they stopped for food on the other side of Perth, it would be a direct ride from there.

'You seem caught in your thoughts, Tavis,' she said now, riding next to him. 'Is all well?'

Startled by her nearness, he shook his head. 'All is well.'

'Have you been here before?' she asked, never taking her eyes from the street or the people making their way along it.

'Once, many years ago with your father.' They skirted a group of people examining the wares in the stalls here in the wool district. 'We were heading to Edinburgh and to meet with the king's ministers about a trade agreement. We passed through here and on to Dundee and then by ship down to Edinburgh. You will like being closer to the sea, Ciara.'

Where the hell had that come from? Good Christ! Would these bits of things remembered about her never cease? She'd always liked the water. Boats.

'James said his home is north of the Tay, before it widens to the sea.'

'Your father travels to Edinburgh several

times a year. It would not be difficult or far for him to visit you here,' he offered.

'He is not my father, Tavis.'

The words made him tense his body and his horse shifted in reaction, pushing them closer to Ciara. She was able to keep hers under control and guided them a pace aside to avoid bumping.

'He raised you as his own, Duncan did.' Safe words since it was commonly known that she was his wife's child.

'If I lasted five years with the Robertsons and just more than ten years with the MacLeries, do you think the Murrays will keep me longer?'

His breath caught at her disclosure and at the sense of hurt and abandonment behind them. Lord Iain's words about her knowledge of her father came back to him and he now saw her curiosity and her accomplishments in a different way.

She was not the confident young woman who had come to him in the night to propose a marriage to him. She was instead an insecure girl who did her best in the hopes of making herself indispensable to her stepfather so that he would keep her.

What could he say? What words could he use

to explain her true worth without then claiming her for himself? Lucky for him, they reached the bridge they needed to cross to leave Perth and he was called away to pay the toll and see to their wagon. By the time they had crossed the bridge and left Perth, Ciara was riding alongside the wagon, chatting with Elizabeth.

Soon, his men returned and they'd brought several others with them.

James Murray was with them.

Tavis hailed them as they approached and stopped his horse to greet the young lord. Instead, James rode past him and stopped before Ciara. Jumping from his horse, he took Ciara's hand and kissed it. And he did not let go while he spoke in hushed tones to only her.

Oh, aye, the Murrays would keep her longer than the MacLeries had, damn them both!

Ciara smiled at James, enjoying the very gallant way he kissed her hand and greeted Elizabeth and Cora, welcoming them to his home. After sharing her weakness with Tavis, she felt vulnerable and exposed. She'd never spoken of such things to anyone, not her mother, not her closest friend. She'd barely admitted them to herself in the darkest hours when self-doubt ruled her thoughts. But this journey was an emotional one as much as it was a business one and her heart ached from all of the truths and changes she faced so far along the way.

'Are you tired from riding, Ciara?' James asked as he mounted once more. His horse was magnificent and her hands itched to take the reins of one like that.

'Nay, my lord,' she replied honestly. 'The roads have been smooth and the skies clear this day.'

He laughed aloud and nodded. Motioning forwards with his head, he asked, 'Would you like to ride ahead with me? It is just a few miles now and my parents await your arrival.'

Ciara turned to look at Tavis, but Cora clucked her tongue before she could.

'That would be a wonderful idea, lass. Go on with the young lord, then, and we will be behind ye.'

'Come then, Ciara,' James said, turning his horse towards the road and nodding. 'You,' he said to Tavis, 'you are in charge?'

'Aye, Lord Murray,' Tavis replied, his tone even though she heard something there.

'See the women and the wagon safely to the keep. At the fork in the road ahead, take the left and go through the village.'

Ciara startled then. She'd never heard Tavis spoken to as though a servant. He sat high in the MacLerie laird's esteem and trust, but to James and others he was simply a servant to order here and there. These lowlanders did not keep to the same practices and sense of family that the clans in the Highlands did.

James smiled at her and she followed him along the road. Though she could have given his horse a good challenge with hers, she paced herself to remain just a bit behind him.

They took the left path at the split and found the village James mentioned to Tavis. James slowed his horse down as they made their way through the narrow street and then spurred it faster once past the cottages, going uphill to the stone keep ahead. Ciara kept her attention on James as the path became steeper, though not truly difficult. It would take some time for the wagon to climb this hill and reach the keep.

The Murrays lived in a stone manor house, built atop the hill and surrounded by a wall. Not knowing what she expected, the unrelenting dark grey was not it. No hint of welcome.

It looked like countless other houses they'd passed, not grand enough to be called castles or true keeps, but walled against intrusion. She wanted to dislike it immediately.

James guided her through the gate and into the small yard in the front. Lord and Lady Murray stood before an open door and waved to her. Ciara waved back and brought her horse to a halt a few yards away. A servant came running to take hold of her horse and James was there at her side to help her down.

Best behaviour. Best behaviour. Best behaviour.

She chanted the words inside her head to remind her of what was expected by her parents and by the laird. It was clear on meeting the Murrays the first time that they disapproved the amount of choice her parents had allowed her and that they should be making the important decisions for her. Ciara caught their glances and narrowing expressions when they were in Lairig Dubh and knew they were looking her over as much as she was them, examining her for defects in character and behaviour. The fact that she hailed from the wild Highlands did not help her cause with them. Shaking the dust from her gown and smoothing it down, she looked up to see James watching her.

'Take a moment to catch your breath, Ciara. That hill tasks even the best of riders,' he whispered as they stood with the horses blocking his parents' view of them. 'Here now, you look lovely.'

Without warning, he leaned down and kissed her. It was nothing but a quick touch on her lips, but it was quite daring for him to do. He stepped back before she could react and held out his arm to her, to escort her to his parents. Ciara met his gaze and smiled, taking his arm and allowing him to lead her.

'Mother. Father. You remember Ciara,' he said, bringing her to the doorway. 'Her companions are behind us and will arrive anon.'

'My lord. My lady,' she said, dropping into a curtsy before them, remaining there a few moments and then rising. 'My thanks to you both for your invitation to visit. My parents and the earl and countess send their greetings and their thanks for your hospitality.'

She might not be Duncan MacLerie's natural daughter, but she was the one who had learned all about being diplomatic from him from the time he brought her home with him from Dunalastair. She listened and watched and learned and could make it through any situation calmly. She would make certain he could be proud of her actions during this trip.

'Come inside, Ciara. The servants will see to your trunks when they arrive,' Lady Murray said, gesturing to her to follow.

Once more the difference between her status as a guest and Tavis's as a MacLerie underling was pointed out to her. His words about that very thing echoed in her mind then and she knew he understood it well.

Lady Murray graciously led her into the house and up to a large chamber on the third floor. It would be for her and Elizabeth while Cora slept in an outer chamber. Her own chamber at her parent's house was half the size and not as luxurious as this. Wherever else they might suffer for lack of gold, they lived in a measure of comfort second to few.

It was the custom to put out the best when entertaining guests, especially when that guest was influential or important. Ciara had no illusions that she was either, but her stepfather and his laird were. The tapestries, though, showed evidence of disrepair when she looked more closely at the edges of them. The bedcoverings showed signs of threadbare areas. The bed and the furniture were worn and in need of repair.

The façade all put in place to impress her enough to follow through with this betrothal and marriage. Her dowry would go far, but exactly for what purposes she did not know. Ciara understood that most believed it mattered not, but it did to her. If she was going to marry someone and make them wealthy, she would like to understand. If she was chattel to be bartered away, she would know the real cost and benefits.

There would be time for all that. For now, she needed to acquaint herself with James and to try to suitably impress his parents and ease the way for this betrothal. Over the last few days, it became clear that she would not fall in love with him. Now, her only goal was to discover if she could tolerate the rest of her life with him.

Tavis guided the rest of the group through the village and up to the manor house at the top of the hill. The wagon moved slowly along and he waited by the side of the pathway for it to pass him. Ciara and James were more than an hour ahead. The urge to grab the boy and grind him into the ground had lessened to a controllable one, for now. If his men had thought anything of his sullen silence they'd not spoken of it or to him.

He knew his duty and he knew how to carry it out and he did not need young James Murray giving him orders.

As they entered the yard, a few men waited for them. They began to unload the wagon, carrying the trunks inside and up to the chamber where Ciara and Elizabeth would stay. They had not brought much with them so it did not take long. Once this task was done, they were directed to a building in the yard at the back of the house where they could eat and sleep.

They had no other duties until Ciara made her decision, so Tavis would make the best of this time by training with his men. And it would give him a chance to work out the anger that bubbled inside him before he had to watch Ciara marry another man—anger at her parents for ever letting her consider a man such as this, but mostly anger at himself for not having the courage to claim her.

Chapter Eight

Tavis did not press Ciara about when they would return to Lairig Dubh. He might have if he'd seen her alone, but he never did. Since the Murrays considered him a servant rather than a guest, he did not have access to the main house without a specific reason. Any information from or about Ciara was passed through Cora and that did not happen often during the next days.

He watched her as she left each morning on a ride with the young Murray. He watched as she and Elizabeth walked through the village. He watched because it was his duty to do so. But Tavis did keep watch carefully so that the Murrays were not insulted by it. That he found it no chore was the part he didn't like to think about much.

Then one day as he and young Iain fought in the yard behind the manor house, he saw her watching him. She wore a deep wine-coloured gown this morning, with no veil covering her long, blonde braid. Without a piece of tartan over her shoulders, she looked like a lowland lass and very much part of this lowland manor. And he guessed that was exactly her aim— to match and to blend in with this family that would be hers soon.

When she laughed and gifted him with a smile as she used to do, the distraction caused him to trip, which then allowed the younger warrior to win their battle and led to much cheering on his part. Laughing at his error, Tavis climbed to his feet and walked to the fence where she stood. Handing his sword off to young Dougal, he accepted a cup of water from her and greeted her.

'You look well, Ciara,' he said, swallowing the water down.

'I am well, Tavis,' she said as she took the cup and tossed it into the water bucket. 'Has there been any news from my father?'

She knew that Duncan would keep in touch

with him during this journey without pressuring her. He nodded.

'And I expect another messenger from him soon. I know that he and Marian arrived home safely.' They'd not gone too far, travelling out to visit one of Connor's other holdings and then back to Lairig Dubh. For appearances, it worked. 'Do you have a letter to send back to him?'

She did not speak at first; instead, she glanced at the manor, then stared off beyond it, as she did when she was calculating the cost of something. Her skills with letters and numbers far surpassed his, but they were helpful to him many times. When she turned back to him, her gaze was filled with that expression of determination he'd seen many times before.

'Send word that we will depart here in three days.'

She was accepting the Murrays' offer.

He knew it in his gut, but when she met his eyes and said nothing more, she confirmed it.

'So, you are accepting this betrothal then?' Tavis leaned down closer so they could not be overheard, all the while knowing this would seal their separate lives. 'Have you told him?'

Ciara blinked several times quickly and he

thought she fought off tears. Looking away to give her time to control herself, he waited, understanding all of the reasons for this match. All of them. And hating each and every one of them.

'Aye. I told James this morn and he is telling his parents even as we speak.'

He inhaled a deep breath and released it. Nodding at her, he said the things he knew she needed to hear. 'His parents approve?'

''Twould seem so. They are overlooking their bloodlines back to the rulers of the ancient kingdom of Moray in accepting me, but their suffering purses are helping them to overlook certain shortcomings.'

'Ciara!' he said, laughing now. She said the most shocking things in a droll voice and it always made him laugh.

For a moment he could hear Lady Murray's nasal tones in the words and he imagined she'd said those words, or some of them, to Ciara already. The same lady Murray who came striding towards them from the house. He stepped away from the fence. 'I will make the arrangements.'

Her hand on his arm stopped him. It felt right and so wrong in the same moment, but he remained within her grasp, giving her a chance to speak.

'Tell me, Tavis. Tell me if you think this a good match.'

The desperate undertones in both the question and in her quivering voice undid him. He was struck by the need to take her in his arms even as his Highland blood urged him to steal her away into the hills to keep her as his own. Instead, for the first of what he knew would be countless times, he carried out his duties to his laird and clan.

'It seems a good match for you, Ciara. You seem of a mind and have many common interests.'

'Horses.'

'And?'

'It matters not, Tavis. We both know it, so do not placate me. I need to know if I can do this.'

'The MacLeries will benefit from the access to this prosperous port and the ability to trade outside of Scotland. The Murrays will get your dowry, which will help them invigorate their farms, villages and lands. James will get a wife who is skilled and educated in all manner of things. And you will get a husband who seems quite pleased to have you as a wife.'

He paused and saw the glimmer of hope in her eyes now. He took the last moment before Lady Murray arrived to finish the hardest task he'd carried out for his clan.

'You can do this. You should do this.'

'There you are, Ciara. James has told us the news and we wish to celebrate with a small feast this night,' Lady Murray gave him a look that spoke of spoiled eels as she glared openly at him. Sliding her arm around Ciara's, she drew her away from the fence and from him. 'Come, we will speak of the meal and of arrangements to accompany you both to your home at Larg…Larg…your home.'

'Lairig Dubh, Lady Murray.' Tavis turned and smiled, for even at her worst moment, Ciara managed somehow to apply humour. 'If you curl your tongue just a bit at the beginning, it is easy enough to pronounce.' She'd begun walking back with her soon-to-be mother-by-marriage, but stopped and glanced back at him.

'My thanks for your wise counsel, Tavis.'

He accepted her thanks with a simple tilt of his head and then watched as the two women made their way back to the manor house to prepare for this celebration.

As the importance of their words sunk in,

frustrated rage began to surge in his blood. He sought out several of the Murray warriors who had been watching him and threw down a challenge to them. Several punishing hours later, when a number of opponents had been laid out in the mud of the yard, he finally gave in to the exhaustion of his body. By then, the celebration in the manor house had begun.

Fortunately for everyone, he had not been invited.

The celebration was not the joyous, large feast she might have expected and, in a way, it fit her mood. Ciara sat at the high table between James and his parents. Cups were raised with cheers for their future happiness. Cups were raised with calls for a fruitful marriage. Cups were raised, but she heard little of the words spoken. The only words that she could think about were those Tavis had spoken to convince her of her path.

Words that said the correct thing, but lacked the sentiment that would have made them the things she needed to hear in that moment. But the same words proved he would carry out his duties and whatever they might wish to be between them was not as important as the greater good. She'd walked back inside to be greeted by a priest and Lord Murray, who'd just signed the betrothal documents from Duncan.

Once it was all done and the betrothal official, she'd begun imbibing. Now, seated next to the man who would claim her as wife in a few short weeks, Ciara emptied the last of the sweet wine in her goblet into her mouth and held it out to a passing servant for more.

'Have a care,' James whispered. 'That wine is more potent than the ale you were drinking.'

Ciara smiled at him and took two mouthfuls in a row, leaving only a sip or two behind. It was, she suspected, the only way to get through this evening. 'My thanks for your concern, James.' She put the cup down and moved it away. 'I am finished.'

He placed his hand on hers where it rested on the edge of the table and his warmth enveloped hers. James met her gaze and the truth of their life together struck her—it would be comfortable. The intensity she always found in Tavis's eyes, the thrill whenever he touched her, even by accident or when he helped her to mount, were lacking in this contact with her betrothed. He would show her affection, he would be caring, he would be considerate, but he would not love her.

She would be what she feared the most—a bride accepted for all that she brought and not find a love match as her parents had.

Ciara remembered Duncan MacLerie's arrival in Dunalastair and how he and her mother met there. She remembered that it was not long before they married and returned to Lairig Dubh and how their love surrounded them always. And, damn her stupid heart, she wanted that for herself. *Could she find it with this man?*

'May I escort you to your chamber?' James asked.

Ciara looked around and realised that both Elizabeth and Cora had asked for leave to retire some time ago and she'd given it. Now that they were formally betrothed, such an act was permitted, so she nodded and stood.

'I will return,' James said to his parents as he walked at her side from the great hall, up the stairs to her room. They continued along the hallway in silence and he stopped before her door. Ciara reached out to lift the latch, but James took her hand in his and drew her close to him.

He slid his hand up to capture her face and

then touched his lips to hers. More than the fleeting kiss a few days ago, this one seemed to be about staking some kind of claim on her. He tilted his head and pressed his mouth against hers, touching her lips with his tongue until she opened to him.

She closed her eyes then, allowing him to lead in this and awaiting the sense of transcendence other women spoke of when this was discussed. His tongue moved into her mouth, seeking hers and touching and tasting it as she did his. James entwined their other hands together, pulling her closer until their bodies touched. He was taller than she and their bodies fitted together nicely.

When he released her hand and wrapped both arms around her, moulding his body to his, Ciara knew there would be no moment of wonder for her. His kissing was pleasant, but did not make her want more or want...anything. The centre of her body that had exploded in heat while watching Tavis naked remained cool and calm. Now, mayhap the wine had dulled her senses and this was much more exciting than she knew?

James loosened his embrace and lifted his head. Pressing a few quick kisses on her cheeks and forehead, he took in a deep breath and re-leased her. Mayhap he had felt it all during this embrace? Had he felt overwhelming desire and longing for her? His eyes, clear and blue, seemed unaffected. Before moving away, he gathered both of her hands in his and kissed them.

'Sleep well, Ciara,' he whispered.

'And you, James,' she replied as she lifted the latch and opened the door to her chamber.

Ciara moved quietly so as to not disturb Cora who, by the sound of the snoring emanating from the pallet in the corner, was asleep already. She began to cross the small antechamber when she realised she'd forgotten her shawl at the table. Since it was one given to her by the laird's wife on the occasion of this journey, she did not want to chance losing it, so crept across the room and quietly made her way out and back along the stairs to the main floor of the house. She reached the great hall and was about to enter when James's voice stopped her before she left the shadows of the corridor.

'She certainly doesn't kiss as I expected the daughter of the Robertson Harlot to kiss.'

Chapter Nine

Ciara's world shattered in that moment. She stumbled back against the wall.

'Blood will out, James, and you will be a lucky man to have that woman warming your bed if her hunger for bedplay is anything like her mother's was.' There was a pause before Lord Murray delivered a most-scathing insult to her mother's reputation. ''Twas said she took three, nay, four men to bed on the night her father found her. Noblemen all, so at least the daughter is of noble blood, even if none would claim her after such a scandal.'

Ciara sucked in a breath so quickly she nearly coughed. She covered her mouth to hide her presence just outside the room.

'The old laird found her naked and wine-soaked, cavorting in his own keep. He could have done worse, but he shaved her head, tossed her out of the keep and banished her for years. Only when the girl was born and raised did the new laird let her back.'

Could they be speaking about her mother? It was unthinkable, of course, but they spoke with such authority. Was this the truth? She roughly rubbed the tears away from her cheeks as she listened to discover more so she could tell the truth from the lies. Surely, they lied?

'I had hoped for more than a whore's daughter for a wife, Father,' James replied to the crude comment made by Lord Murray that had her shaking so badly she nearly lost her balance. 'Not a wife who will cuckold me with any man when I am not there.'

'We need the dowry, James. You know that,' Lord Murray explained. 'And the connections to her uncle and her stepfather.'

'Aye, Father. I know it. It will be the difference between complete failure and success.'

'Virgin or not matters not in this. The daughter of a whore or a saint matters not. The laird promised she is an innocent, but I doubt it with the way that guard sniffs around her. But even that matters not,' Lord Murray explained calmly.

They believed her so dishonourable and yet accepted her for marriage into their family? His next words made his priority clear.

'So take the benefits you gain from this marriage and enjoy them. A young man like you will find many uses for a woman like that one. May you and your cock be strong enough to survive the nights with her in your bed!'

Goblets clinked as though touched in a toast and Ciara heard the chairs scrape along the stone floor. They were leaving. Ciara glanced around and found a small alcove set back in the wall, so she pressed herself into it and waited for them to walk past her.

It felt like forever as she tried to unravel what was truth and what was deceit in the words she had heard. Ciara stood silent in the darkness a good while after the sound of their footsteps passed and moved off to their chambers. She was undone by it all. Shocked past action or clear thought, she simply waited to see if it made sense if she allowed a few minutes to fade away.

And another few minutes.

And another.

Was this why her parents had avoided accompanying her here? Was it more than simply trying to give more credence to a possible betrothal than they wanted to? Did they worry that their presence would stir up such talk from a rumoured past?

Thoughts and old memories swirled inside her mind until she wanted to scream. If it were daytime, she would ride, for it always cleared her thoughts and helped her to think. Mayhap she should ask Elizabeth, nay, Cora, about the truth of it? But how could she bring up such matters as the ones she'd heard spoken of by James and his father? Elizabeth was her age and would not remember discussions or mention of such things. Cora had been the laird's wife's servant for many years and would not reveal something she'd been ordered not to tell.

That left only one person whom she could trust.

Tavis.

Could he know the truth of it? Would he have kept it from her all these years if he knew it?

Ciara peeked out of the shadows and searched for signs or noises of nearby servants or guests. Finding none, she went by way of the kitchens and storage rooms and out into the yard. The forgotten shawl would be helpful now as the night air chilled, but she was not going back for it. She skirted around the main barracks to a smaller building where she knew that Tavis and his men stayed. So intent on discovering the truth of her past was she that she never looked up and never saw Tavis standing in the dark right next to her path. Only when she began to lift the door's latch did he stop her.

'Ciara, where are you going?' Tavis asked.

His words, his voice, scared her and she leapt back, dropping her hands to her sides. It took a few moments to find the breath she'd lost.

'I was looking for you, Tavis. I need to… speak to you privately,' she said; her voice trembled with every word she spoke and she could not stop it. How would she ever get the questions out? How would she speak about the terrible things she'd heard?

'We did this once and things did not turn out well between us. Mayhap you should sleep on this matter and we can speak on the morrow?' he said, moving a few paces away from her.

The one thing she'd never considered in all their dealings was that he had known the truth and that was why he did not accept her proposal of marriage. Now, looking at his discomfort, it seemed the most likely explanation to her.

'You could have at least spoken the truth to me, Tavis,' she whispered. He seemed to pale at her accusation, but it was difficult to tell in the dark. She wondered now if she wasn't on to the truth at the heart of it all. 'You could choose not to marry the daughter of a whore, but James is so desperate that he must and will.'

Her heart broke in that moment when he did not deny her accusations. He'd been her first and most stalwart friend and yet he had never revealed the most basic truth of her life to her—who she truly was.

She turned to leave, to flee, to find some place of peace where she could think and reason her way through the myriad of feelings racing through her heart and her soul, when he grabbed her by the arm and pulled her close to him.

'You know that is not true, Ciara. I would have accepted, but there are too many reasons I cannot,' he argued in a quiet voice.

She glanced up at his face, trying to search for some sign of certainty, but saw none there. He wore that face of stone, one devoid of all emotion, the very one she hated every time it lay on his face.

'So, you do not deny that they spoke the truth of my past?'

He let out a breath and shook his head. 'I…'

'Why? Why did you keep such things from me?' she asked, feeling the last vestiges of her control slipping away. She took a step back and shrugged off his hold. 'I thought…I thought…'

At that moment she did not know what to think, so she did not. Instead, she lifted the edges of her gown and ran. She ran from him, from the hurtful words and insults she'd heard and from his betrayal of her trust. She ran from whatever the truth was. She just ran.

The gates were yet open, so she slipped through and followed the road into the village. Once there, she remembered a small stream that began nearby and grew into a river that fed into the Tay estuary. There was a small clearing and she found it a few minutes later. Ciara dropped on to a fallen log and tried to catch her breath.

As her thoughts tumbled around in her mind and as she searched her memories for any that would have warned her of such matters, she knew she would have to face Tavis and discover his reasons for joining in the deception that counted now as her whole life.

The peace and quiet of the night belied the turmoil within her. The melodic sounds of the birds of night, calling out from high in the trees, should have soothed her. But not this night. Not even the puffy clouds moving slowly over the face of the moon would do that. Not even... The sound of his steps through the bush behind her warned of his approach before she saw him near.

'Tavis,' she whispered his name as he walked to where she sat.

He did not try to come closer, treating her like a skittish colt that was ready to kick out and flee. Instead he spoke quietly and sat on a large rock, across the small clearing from her. He thrust a torch he carried into the ground, allowing them to see each other more clearly in the dark.

'It is not safe for you out here alone, Ciara.'

'Not safe for the daughter of a slut or not safe for the woman raised as something and some-one she is not?'

He winced at the anger and betrayal in her voice. But then he had played his part in this and he knew she felt betrayed by him more than probably even her parents.

'Ciara, you were raised by two parents who love you and given everything a young woman of noble blood would have—an education, opportunities to travel and use your knowledge.' She glared at him then and he took the anger better than the betrayed expression.

'He said that my mother was called the Robertson Harlot. He said that she was found with three or four men in her bed. He said...' she paused then and he heard the emotion in her voice and knew she must be crying '...he said that no one knows who my father is.'

Understanding how deeply she felt about Duncan and how this must cut her deeply, he wondered how to answer her. Tavis knew some of it because he'd been there with Duncan when his marriage to Marian had happened. Even young, in that awkward time between youth and manhood, he understood the gossip at that time and knew Marian had a terrible reputation and that their marriage had been forced by her brother. The reasons had never been shared with him.

Then, the same brother, Laird Iain, had ordered him not to tell her anything of her past, his voice filled with fear that he might actually know something more than he should. Connor and Duncan had never spoken of it, but the matter had not been mentioned in Lairig Dubh since that first night they arrived by the MacLerie's own orders. Now faced with the haunted look in her eyes and his part in what she counted as betrayal, he thought about what he should tell her.

'I think he fell in love with you first, Ciara,' Tavis said, remembering back to the days after their arrival in Dunalastair and Duncan's request for the first of the carved animals. 'He met you and you made him think of all he'd never had—a family, bairns, a place of his own. He did not mention your mother to me at all when he asked for the horse.'

It was the truth. Duncan spoke only of a little blonde lass with huge brown eyes who loved horses. Of how he wanted to give her something to play with, something that would make her smile, something to please her. Only later did Duncan ever mention Marian, or Mara as she was then called.

'Duncan became your father and has never been less than that. You know that in your heart.'

'Was my mother a wh—?' She could not seem to finish the word.

'There were rumours she was.'

The words damned her mother no matter how softly he spoke them or how unadorned they were.

'But from the moment I met her, she never acted dishonourably. And from the time she spoke the joining words and handfasted with Duncan and entered our clan, the Robertson Harlot was never spoken of again.'

Ciara rubbed her eyes with the back of her hand, smearing the tears more than she wiped them away. 'So everyone but me knows this story?'

'I am sorry, Ciara. The rumours about your mother were widespread at the time. Come now, you know how a scandal is spoken of and it grows and grows. It was the gossip at the time and little else challenged it.'

'Why did they not reveal this to me instead of this farce? Did they hope that I would never learn about their lies and deception?'

'Ciara,' he whispered, his voice echoing in the quiet surrounding them, 'they hoped that their beloved daughter would never be hurt by mean gossip. They hoped that you could find a match you could accept.' He would have gone on, but she held up her hand to stop him.

'If he, if they loved me the way you say they do, they would have told me the truth so that I would not be hurt in finding out from strangers. But what hurts me more, Tavis, is that you never told me these things when you knew about them.'

He winced at her accusation. A true one, but there had never been a time to speak about personal matters. First she was too young and knew not of such things. Then she was grown and, again, it was not for him to tell her. But she was caught up in the hurt and could not consider that now.

'I found out from strangers who want only my dowry and from a man who counselled his son on the benefits of having a harlot's daughter in his bed...even if my kiss was less than satisfying.'

He stood then and his fists began to curl and uncurl as she said that. The young whelp had insulted her so? She was an innocent and the Murrays were unhappy with that? They both needed to be pounded into the ground for allowing her to hear such things.

'I understand this all now,' she said, though

he doubted that was correct. 'Only an inde-
cently large dowry would overcome the objections of most families when invited to have
their sons marry a woman like me. So, my
uncle provided part and Duncan the other, in
the hopes of marrying me off as quickly as
possible.'

'Ciara, you are hurt. Your words are from
that anger.' He knew it since he'd done the same
thing since realising there was more between
them than he'd thought or admitted before. He
convinced himself that she would calm down,
but her next words showed him otherwise.

'They care not if I come to this marriage innocent or used.'

Tavis met her gaze and found it desolate.
God help him, he wanted to wipe away the
pain and hurt there. He was on his feet before
he thought to move and sat next to her, gathering her in his arms to comfort her with nothing more than simple compassion as his intent.

He brushed the hair from her face as she
cried against his chest. Though usually the
most clear-thinking of lasses, this went deeper
than simple insult. This would feed the need
inside her now to believe she was worthless.
Why had Duncan and Marian not prepared her

for this? Regardless of orders to the contrary, Tavis knew what must be done.

'I travelled with your father to negotiate a treaty with your uncle. It was my first time and I was so full of myself,' he said, laughing a bit at the memory. 'I was the youngest, yet even I had heard about the stories. Duncan warned us not to speak of such things since it was about the new laird's sister.'

She stopped crying as hard then and Tavis knew she was listening.

'Aye, the stories were bad, but even we knew they were not all true. Good stories seem to go their way, but bad ones grow as they're passed and there was no doubt these had been.'

'What had you heard?' she whispered, tilting her back a bit so she could look at him.

'Just what Lord Murray said—she was a whore, was in bed with a number of men, her father banished her for dishonouring her clan and that you were born.'

'And Duncan married her?'

'I was not privy to the more personal matters, but, aye, Duncan handfasted with her before we left Dunalastair and they had a church wedding the next spring. Your sister was born later that year.'

'How did they keep this all secret from me, Tavis? If so many know, how did I not?'

'Ah, lass. The first night when we arrived back in Lairig Dubh, when the hall was rife with gossip and all the stories, Connor made things very clear. He stood behind your mother and acknowledged her marriage to Duncan and claimed her for the clan MacLerie. Said any insult to her was an insult to all.'

'And that was all he said?' She leaned back now and he missed the warmth of her against him.

'Ah, but Connor did it in his best *beast of the Highlands* voice. The one he uses to frighten people into obedience. No one dares the beast!'

'Jocelyn does.'

'She never believed the rumours about him being a murderous beast.' He let those words hang in the silence between them, letting Ciara make the connection.

'So you think my mother was not a whore? That these were all just rumours and stories?' she asked. A hopeful tone filled her voice now and he feared giving her the wrong impression. Tavis did not know the truth about Marian before he met her. Her actions since that time were unquestionably honourable. Was that because she'd left behind her scandalous life that had led to the rumours?

'Only your mother and Duncan know the truth of it, but soon after they handfasted, another clan came from a distance seeking the truth about you.'

'Me?' She sat back and shrugged. 'Why would they ask?'

'Rumours beget rumours and there were many about the old Robertson laird's family. Duncan swore that you were hers before the whole clan and the other laird and claimed you as his own.'

Tavis did not need to tell her the whole of it for it would bring up more questions. Questions he could not answer. Damn Duncan and Marian for not explaining this all to her when she came to a marriageable age!

'I have felt some of this all my life, Tavis. That I did not belong here. That I was not worthy. Now I understand why I am to be passed hand to hand—a bastard born of no family and wanted by none.'

There was an instant when he knew he should stop and simply return her to the house. When they should talk more in the cool light of the morn, but that moment passed by so quickly it did not hinder his next action at all. Tavis pulled her back into his arms, tilted her head with his hand and leaned his mouth to hers.

'Never think that, Ciara. Never,' he whispered as he kissed her and all his good intentions to show simple compassion were tossed asunder at the first touch of his mouth on hers.

He kissed her with all the longing in his body and heart. He kissed her with the respect and liking he felt for her. He kissed her for all the wanting and knowing he could never have her. He kissed her.

Not as a beginning as the young Murray had, but as an ending because her place, her life, would be here and not with him.

And though the way she whispered his name as he lifted his mouth from hers made him want to hear it again and again and to hear it whispered in the deepest moment of joining, he knew it for what it was—the last time he would hear it spoken in that manner. He righted her and then stood. Reaching down for the torch, he did the hardest thing he had ever done.

'Come, Ciara,' he said, holding out his hand to her. She touched her fingers to her lips and then met his gaze.

'Where are you taking me, Tavis?' she asked.

In words that would damn him in her eyes, he remembered his honour and hers and replied, 'Back to the house. If Elizabeth comes looking for you, she will raise more questions.'

Her gazed narrowed and then her eyes widened and he knew the moment she understood. If she thought he was declaring his love for her, and he suspected that was exactly what she thought, this would end any dreams of such a thing happening.

'But you kissed me. You want me,' she challenged.

'Aye, I do, but I cannot have you. Too much depends on this marriage of yours to the Murray heir. I will not dishonour your word or mine.'

She lifted her hand up to slap his face and he waited for the sting. He deserved it. Instead she placed it gently there and caressed his cheek. 'He already thinks we have.'

Stunned by that, he stepped back and motioned to the path back to the gates. 'I will not take that step, then, to confirm him right. You will prove him wrong on your wedding night,' he said.

Confusion filled her gaze now and Tavis comprehended that any more words spoken would worsen the situation, not help it. As he guided her back to the gates and then waited in the shadows for her to go in alone, he cursed himself with every foul word he knew. He fought a battle within his soul over the right thing to do for her, for him and for what could not be between them. He was not worthy of her for so many reasons. Reasons that could not simply go away because he wanted her or he'd kissed her. Reasons that haunted his heart and soul every day that he drew breath. In the end, Tavis understood that he was damned, no matter what.

Chapter Ten

The sun shone brightly and everyone saw to their daily tasks, but Ciara remained abed. When Elizabeth questioned her, she blamed it on a sour stomach and head pains. Cora then wisely declared that she should not overindulge in wine if she wished to avoid such a condition. She banished them all from the chamber, only to find that, one by one, they returned. Worse, Lady Murray visited with a family remedy for such things.

Its foul odour reached her before the lady handed her the cup and her stomach, so far not truly in distress, began to retch. She drank it down without complaint, fearing that to do so would only prolong the lady's visit. Soon, the brew brought on sleep, which could not be a bad thing considering that she'd not slept at all the night before.

Her sleep filled with images of that kiss and she lived it over and over again in those dreams. The passionate way he whispered to her as he touched his lips to hers. Then he consumed her with his mouth, tasting and caressing her lips and tongue with his until she could not breathe or think.

Ciara had been kissed before, but nothing had prepared her for the overwhelming, breath-stealing heat that filled her blood and melted the centre of her. Her body wanted him, her heart ached for him and her soul hoped against hope that this would be the step that changed everything between them.

He admitted that he wanted her and his mouth promised such pleasure as he claimed her. She whispered his name when he lifted his face from hers and closed her eyes, awaiting the next touch, the next kiss…the moment when he would claim her as his and set themselves against whoever would deny his right to her.

When the reality followed the dream and she realised he had turned his back on her just as everyone important in her life had, she fought her way out of the troubled sleep. Her body ached as the dream faded, leaving behind the memories of their kiss. Accepting that the moment was over, Ciara opened her eyes.

Unfortunately, when she did, she found James sitting at her bedside. She nearly laughed when she noticed Elizabeth sitting in the far corner sewing some torn garments. She knew that Elizabeth was there partly to protect her reputation—laughable now, but she did not know that—or so as not to miss anything interesting that might happen.

'Ah, you are awake,' he said quietly.

Ciara shifted on the bed, pulling the covers up to mask the fact that she yet wore her gown from yesterday. And she glanced away, trying to banish the memories of the taste and feel of Tavis from her before speaking to James.

'Aye. The potion your mother gave me made me sleep longer. Is it mid-day yet?' she asked, noticing how bright the chamber was from the light pouring in through the window. She pushed herself back up to sit against the wooden headboard, tugging the bedcovers higher as she moved and then gathering her loosened hair behind her shoulders.

'Past mid-day,' he said. 'Elizabeth, you said

Cora had made some tea for Ciara. Would you get it now?'

Nicely dismissed, Elizabeth nodded to him and gifted Ciara with an expression that promised retribution for anything missed. She did leave the door open as she left, something that amused her now. Once they were alone, James took her hand in his.

'I feared that this illness was my fault for pressing my affections on you last evening,' he said. 'I apologise if it is.'

Ciara studied him as he spoke. She had never been one to play games and hide the truth. She had sought to use candour rather than deception. So she decided that she would be honest with him in this and set the practice for their life together, now that it was clear to her there would be one.

'It was not the kissing, James, but rather what I overheard after that in the hall.'

She waited and watched for his reaction. It came swiftly—he paled and could not meet her gaze. Then he stood and began to pace the chamber as though seeking the words to explain. When he did not speak soon enough, she did.

'I had never heard those rumours until you and your father spoke of them.'

'Ciara...I...' He stumbled over the words. She raised her hand and shook her head to stop him from more.

'I cannot answer about my mother's past— whore or not, I do not know,' she said. A loud crash interrupted from the outer chamber. Clearly, Elizabeth was listening and trying to pour the tea and had dropped the pot. James closed the door then, keeping this conversation between them.

'But I have only been as I was raised to be and can only speak about my behaviour. If you have questions about it, ask me now so that no misunderstanding exists between us.'

He stopped and stared at her, then blinked several times. 'You are unlike any other woman I know, Ciara.' His blue eyes were serious as they met hers.

'Clearly. For good or bad, this is who I am.' She pushed back the bedcovers and slid to the edge of the bed. He glanced in surprise at her gown, but did not mention it aloud. 'Your words so shocked and hurt me I sought answers from the only person who could answer them for me.'

'The man who brought you here?'

'Aye. Tavis is an old friend and I sought his counsel.'

She'd sought much more, but that was over. He'd returned her to James Murray and ended any possibility of anything else. His face darkencd, most likely remembering his father's suspicions. But he did not ask.

'I'd thought myself in love with him from the time I was a child, James. My parents asked him to see me safely here to you. He is a family friend and nothing more.' She hoped the words, spoken aloud, would convince both of them. But in her heart, she screamed out in anger at Tavis's dismissal of what truly was between them and his reasons for keeping them apart. James seemed to think about her words before nodding his acceptance.

'Ciara, I did not mean to question your honour,' James began. 'But with what my father had told me from the beginning and knowing that you seek him out, I doubted you.' A knock warned of intrusion and the door began to open. Elizabeth carried a cup before her.

'Leave us,' Ciara said. Elizabeth nodded and pulled the door closed. Standing, she walked to face him. 'No matter my mother's past, no matter what rumours you might hear otherwise, you will find me pure on our marriage night.'

His eyes widened and then he smiled. 'That pleases me, Ciara.' He lifted her hands and kissed one, then the other. 'I think I like this candour between us.'

'I cannot promise there will not be conflict between us, James, but I can promise it will never happen because of dishonesty on my part.'

She could tell he wanted to test her with a kiss, but he decided otherwise and stepped back, releasing her hands. He lifted the latch on the door and opened it. Elizabeth moved quickly away and waited to be asked in.

'Elizabeth, see to your friend's comfort,' James said with a nod to her. 'I hope to see you at the evening meal, if you are feeling up to it.'

The door from the outer chamber to the hall had not closed for a second before Elizabeth thrust the cup in her hands, placed her hands on her hips and demanded the truth from her.

'What did he say about your mother?' she asked.

Ciara sipped the tea. It would soothe her as it always did. And it would give her a few moments to work out what to say to her friend.

'Well? I could not have heard what I think I heard? Tell me!' she ordered as she clenched her jaw shut and ground out the words. Elizabeth strode over to the bed and threw herself on it, rolling on her stomach and leaning on her elbows.

'I overheard James speaking to his father about his misgivings about our marriage last evening.' That was a good beginning. Elizabeth would take the lead and drag the rest of it out now.

'When? I was at the feast with you.'

'After you retired, James escorted me back and he kissed me.'

Elizabeth sighed, clearly enamoured of this betrothal. Tavis was, as she'd told Ciara many times, too old for her. She liked James because he was only a few years older than either of them. And he was not as intimidating as Tavis. The sight of a naked Tavis, though it had excited Ciara, had overwhelmed Elizabeth. She would have to begin searching through the Murray men for an appropriate husband for her dear friend.

'Was it wonderful?' she asked, closing her eyes as she did.

'It was…nice.'

Elizabeth rolled over on to her side and gave Ciara a perplexed glance. 'Nice? But that is good, is it not?'

Ciara did not want nice, she wanted more than that. She wanted a kiss from her future husband to be wonderful and exciting and transcendent. Like Tavis's later kiss was. Rather than trying to explain it, she simply agreed.

'Aye. But I realised afterwards I'd forgotten my shawl on my chair and went back to get it.'

'That one? The one James brought with him earlier?' Ciara nodded, embarrassed that she'd not even noticed it.

'I was about to enter the hall when I heard them talking about my mother.'

Elizabeth might seem like a flighty young girl when they spoke of a kiss, but she was her closest friend and she knew this was a serious matter. She moved to Ciara's side and drew her to sit next to her on the bed, holding tightly on to her hand and not letting go.

'I had no inkling of any of it,' she whispered, the words and truth still difficult to accept let alone speak of it to another. 'My mother was called the Robertson Harlot.'

It made no sense to her even now that Tavis had confirmed it. Marian Robertson a whore?

Her mother never even looked at another man and was deeply in love with Duncan. She shook her head. 'I cannot believe it, but Tavis confirmed it.'

'You spoke to Tavis about this? When?' Elizabeth asked as she pressed a linen square in her hand.

Ciara did not even realise that tears flowed once more. She dabbed her eyes and then tried to tell the rest.

'I listened until they left the hall and could not even believe all they'd said. I went to find Tavis, hoping he would tell me it was all a lie,' Ciara said. Taking in and releasing a deep breath, she admitted the painful truth to her friend. 'My mother was found with several men by her father and banished as punishment. She bore me during that exile and was only allowed back after I was born.'

Elizabeth gasped then. 'It cannot be true, Ciara. It cannot.' She shook her head several times. 'Your mother and father...'

'I always knew Duncan was my stepfather and never knew about my real father. I was but a bairn the few times I asked and even I understood it was not to be asked again. I asked again just before we left Lairig Dubh, but my mother said we would speak of such things when we had time.' She shook her head and Elizabeth tsked several times in sympathy.

'Apparently what my mother does not wish me to know is that no one knows which of those several men is the one.' Elizabeth released her hand and jumped up from the bed.

'Tavis said this is true?'

'He said that he did not know if it was the truth, but he heard the same rumours when he accompanied Duncan to Dunalastair when he met my mother. And that my mother never denied it. The laird declared that it was past and that none in Lairig Dubh were to speak of it.'

'Surely your parents would have told you if this were the truth? They would have to expect you'd hear this.'

'Mayhap they hoped that the Murrays were so desperate they would not bring up such a shameful matter and insult either the MacLeries or the Robertsons?' she pointed out. 'I cannot ask them anything until I return. But it is too late now to rescind my agreement to marry James.'

'Why would you change your mind? Did he offer you some insult?' Elizabeth crossed her arms over her chest and lifted her chin a bit.

'Let me speak to him and I will make certain he knows these are lies.' Her staunchest supporter, always ready to protect and defend her.

'James and I are at peace over this, Elizabeth. He appreciated my frankness in speaking to him about the matter, so there is no need for you to provoke him in any way.'

'And Tavis? Where does he stand in all this?'

Ciara turned her head and looked away. He had kissed her with abandonment, showing her everything that James's kiss was not, and then sent her back to him. He expected her to stand by the betrothal and live her life without him. He had convinced himself that he could not claim her for himself and no matter how or what she argued, his reasons stood in their way. Damn the man!

'He returned me to the Murrays, but not before showing me that he does feel something for me. A taste of what passion is like.'

Elizabeth gasped then. 'What did he do?'

''Twas only a kiss,' she explained, trying to believe it herself. Instead her body remembered the heat and the thrill once more, leaving her breathless in its power.

He returned *you to James*.

The reality of that action cooled her immediately. Anger flared now that he could claim she meant something to him and then he could discard her in the next moment.

'A moment of passion that is gone now. Do not worry. He said there are reasons, but goes no further,' she explained. Ciara looked at her friend and shared her innermost worries about everything she'd learned last night.

'I think that this hidden truth, whatever it is, is the reason why the MacLeries are so happy to rid themselves of me. My uncle provided most of my dowry, I know that much, so it costs them little and gains them much. Since the Murrays are in great need, this works out for them. James marries me for my dowry and the truth as he knows it does not stand in the way.' She paused and took a breath.

'Tavis has some truth that stands in his way and he will not reveal it. My parents live with some lie that they will not reveal. And I stand in the middle of it, gaining a husband who does not want me, losing a man who does and with parents and family who do not care enough to give me the truth.'

Elizabeth threw her arms around her then and hugged her to within an inch of her life, forcing almost all the air from her lungs.

'None of that matters, Ciara. You are a jewel and James Murray understands that or I will beat it into him!' she promised. 'Once they discover all of your skills and talents, once they know you better, the Murrays will know they had the best part of this bargain.'

Elizabeth retrieved Ciara's brush and began to ease it through her hair. There was silence between them for several minutes.

'You have spoken of everyone involved in this except yourself, Ciara. What of you and your feelings?'

'I know not,' she admitted with a shrug. 'Within just a few weeks, my entire world has turned. My parents are not who I believed them to be. A man I thought did not love me may indeed have feelings for me, but he says he cannot claim me. And now I am betrothed to a man I know I will not love. At this moment, I do not think I feel anything at all.'

But try as she might to deny feeling anything, the flames of anger did burn within her. Anger at—

The knock at the door startled them. Cora opened the door and looked from one to the other the way her mother or Elizabeth's mother did when she caught them doing something wrong or unseemly. They laughed this time with an ease built on their long friendship. With a warning not to be late for the evening meal and a telling glance at the already-worn gown, Cora closed the door and left them to themselves.

'The next few weeks are set,' Elizabeth explained as she helped Ciara off with the now slept-in gown and searched for a clean one. 'You will know nothing more until we return to Lairig Dubh and speak to your parents. So, take this time to become accustomed to James. If the marriage is a certainty...' She paused and looked at her, waiting. At Ciara's nod, she continued, 'Then it hurts nothing to learn more about him and prepare yourself.'

'He does seem willing to accept me in spite of believing the worst about my mother and father,' she offered.

Elizabeth slipped the clean gown, one in a paler shade of green, over her head and tied the laces of it. 'That is to his credit, then. And if he already thinks this sordid tale is the truth, then you have nothing to worry over.'

Ciara nodded, allowing her friend to think that.

But there was something worse—if given

but a sign by Tavis last night, she would have given away her honour for the chance to lie in his arms just once before she belonged to another man.

He had not dreamt of her in years, at least four, even though the very thought of her and his failure to save her as he'd promised plagued him daily. Saraid filled his dreams that night, not the pleading one, not the one who laid her death at his feet, but the one with whom he fell in love so many years ago.

They walked the hills and paths around Lairig Dubh, laughing and learning each other. Already betrothed and only weeks until they were wed, they spent the time doing what couples in love did—testing the limits of their resolve. He would never dishonour her, no matter the hunger he had for her in his body and his heart. They would have the rest of their lives to love each other and if they spent every moment in their bed, he would not complain.

Saraid was a few yards in front of him and she began to run. It would take him no effort to catch her, but this was a game they played, drawing it out and the winner demanding a forfeit from the other. Many, many kisses had been won or lost during their afternoon together and he hoped for many more. Now, she scampered away from him and he ran a couple of paces and caught her, pulling her close and demanding his prize.

She kissed him with such ferocity it surprised him. Not that she did not enjoy this game, he knew she did, but she rarely controlled their kissing. He liked it when she did, for he glimpsed the passion that waited deep inside her. For him and only him. This time as he tasted her mouth, slipping his tongue inside hers and holding her close, she guided his hand up over the fullness of her breast and arched against his touch.

In only weeks, he could claim her as his.

Then, she lifted her mouth from his and touched his cheek. Saraid smiled and whispered to him, *'If anything happens to me, you must go on.'*

Tavis shook his head. *'Nothing will happen. We will be happy together for our lives.'* He kissed her again to convince her.

'Promise me. Promise me, Tavis,' she urged.

'I promise.'

Tavis woke in the middle of saying the words. He sat up on the rough pallet where he slept and pushed the hair out of his face. Looking around, he was glad none of the others had heard him speak in his sleep. He stood, threw the length of plaid around him and walked outside. The shades of dawn were just creeping into the sky and soon the birds would awaken and begin their call to start the day.

He stood in the quiet and tried to slow his racing heart and breathing down. It felt so real to him, as though Saraid had been there, as though he had been kissing her and touching her as they had in the past. And the words, the promise, were ones he'd forgotten, but now remembered giving her that day.

She would jest about the bad things that happened to her family and how she had a feeling that they followed her as well, awaiting a time and place to happen. A chill traced up and down his spine as he realised she had known her future that day. Her death would always be on his conscience. If only he had not pressed her to attend the gathering with him. If only he'd not left in anger. If only... Tavis shook off the past and thought about the promise he'd long forgotten.

If anything happens to me, you must go on. He searched his memory, wondering if she'd spoken them or if his guilty conscience was now serving his own needs. Now that he thought about it, he realised she'd said those same words to him a number of times after that as well.

As the sun finally rose, which it had been threatening to for as long as he'd been standing there, he decided that he would ask Connor to be assigned to another of his properties in the north. He could no longer walk those same paths and live each day in the places where his worst failures as a man yet lived. He would see Ciara safely back to her parents, explain his failures to Connor and then live elsewhere until he figured out what his future should be.

Realising that he stood there with only a plaid tossed over his shoulders, he turned to go back inside to dress for the day. And he would have if the young Murray was not walking straight towards him with a purpose clear in his intense expression.

Chapter Eleven

'I would have words with you, MacLerie,' the young lord said as he approached.

He tipped his head to the young man and then motioned to his condition. 'Shall I dress before this talk, my lord?'

James finally noticed his state of undress and waved him off in that imperious way that he had. 'I will wait.'

Tavis did not rush, but he did not dawdle, either, and returned to find James examining their horses inside the fenced yard.

'She is quite skilled at riding,' James said. 'That black is a beast.'

'Aye, she is. Has been since early on,' Tavis added, standing at the young man's side as the horses moved around the enclosure.

'How long have you known her?'

'She had but five years,' Tavis said. 'A wee thing with big brown eyes. She reminded me of my youngest sister at the time.'

'And now you protect her?' he asked.

Uncertain of his goal, Tavis nodded. 'At her parents' and the laird's request.'

'What is your position with the earl?'

'I command his personal guards and work with Rurik Erengislsson, the commander of all his soldiers.' Tavis turned and faced the man. 'Why not just ask the questions you wish to ask, my lord?'

'Why?' The words tumbled out then. 'Why does she seek you out?'

'I eased her way in her journey from Dunalastair to Lairig Dubh. I befriended her when there was no one else. She knows I will protect her even now.'

'That is my job now, MacLerie.'

'Aye, it will be when the words are spoken. Until then, I carry out my duty to my laird and the lass.'

James nodded at him and began to walk away, then he stopped and came back. 'I had no intention of revealing something so painful to her. I meant no insult to her or your laird.'

Tavis meant to let him leave without another word, but he could not stop himself, it seemed. The young man was not a bad one, just young, and Tavis could see much of himself in him when he was that age.

'I do not stand in your way in this betrothal or your marriage to her,' he offered. No matter his own wants or needs, he would do his duty.

The young Murray accepted his words with a nod and then seemed to have another question he did not know how to ask. 'Is there something else, my lord?'

'Have you fought in battles, MacLerie?'

'Aye, my lord, I have. And nearly been killed in a couple of them.' He had come close a few times. Luckily one of his cousins or another had his back as he had theirs and they had walked out with some wounds and a few scars.

'I have watched you fighting, training, with your men. I would join you...'

'We will be here after we break our fast, my lord. 'Tis your house and your yard. None would object to working with you,' he said.

The young lord ran off then and Tavis was struck by the strangeness of the situation. In the moments when he allowed bitterness to fill his heart, he hated the man for being the one who would claim Ciara. He despised that James Murray would take her to his bed, make her his own, and be the one who commanded her life and her future. He hated…

Shaking his head, Tavis turned back to watch the horses run. But as the young lord's actions had just now proven, he was not a bad man. He had offered an apology for speaking of better-left-unsaid matters and had tried to settle things between them, understanding that Tavis was in some way important to Ciara.

Older, better men than he would not have attempted such things or admit that their behaviour had offered insult in some way, so Tavis allowed a begrudging measure of respect for those actions, though he did not like feeling even that towards him. James Murray was as much a pawn in this as was Ciara and even himself, so the fact that he faced a man he suspected of inappropriate attentions to his betrothed and believed his explanation, and hers, spoke well of him, too.

His men began to rouse now, as did the rest of the household. His plan was to train until mid-day and then prepare for the journey back to Lairig Dubh that would begin on the morrow. After their meal, he called them into the yard and they paired off with sword or axe and targe. James did join them and, though clearly inexperienced at true battles, held his own in the mock battles.

When Tavis glanced up and noticed Ciara watching them, he wondered if she thought one of them would kill the other and he wondered for which one she would cheer. Understanding that it was ill advised to defeat the Murray heir in front of his family and those who served him, Tavis held in the frustrations he ached to unleash on the man who would claim Ciara and allowed James to win their match.

But only just.

'Are they daft?' Ciara said aloud. She'd thought it for some time as she watched them training in the yard.

'They are being men,' Cora advised from behind.

They were walking, enjoying the clear, sunny morning when she'd spotted them near the enclosure where their horses were. Ciara thought to ride a bit on her last morning here, to exercise her horse and stretch her own muscles in preparation for the journey home, only to find James and Tavis and most of the Murrays and all of the MacLeries fighting there. Even Lord Murray stood watching, calling out suggestions and cheering on his son and his men as the battle went in one direction or another.

There seemed to be rules—once a man was knocked off his feet, he left the field. No killing or maiming blows, though she could not be certain that none were injured. Blood flowed, she could see it even at this distance, for most of them fought bare-chested. Before she knew it, she was just a few paces away from the edge of it, holding her breath as only Tavis and James remained in the centre. Though there were far fewer MacLeries, those men were no less boisterous in cheering on their man than the outnumbering Murrays were.

Then, in a move she'd not seen before, Tavis seemed to grab James's sword with his and fling it into the air and away. James, who had lost his dagger as well and was now weaponless, charged at Tavis and, at the last moment, kicked out his leg and tripped him to the ground. The Murrays cheered loudly, running to congratulate James and to pull Tavis up.

How did men do it? How could they be bitter rivals one moment and friends the next? She shook her head and watched as Tavis counselled James on the move he'd used to disarm him and then let him practise it several times on him. Soon they were practising it and sharing battle moves with each other's men.

Ciara, Elizabeth and Cora left them behind to finish their practice and went back to begin packing. Lady Murray's maids were already preparing her trunks, they'd been told, and Ciara expected that the trip back would take much longer than it had taken to get here. But there would be company for the journey and Lady Murray had even made arrangements for them to stay with relatives along the way so that they would be more comfortable.

Or she would be more comfortable!

Their party would now be four wagons, along with a score of Murray guards and more with the MacLeries mixed in to round out the count to almost two score in total.

A small army, Ciara thought as she mounted the next morning and watched as the whole entourage began to clamour out of the yard, through the village towards the main road. Lady Murray preferred to ride in the wagon, so hers had been fitted with comfortable, cushioned seats and Cora had taken refuge within it. Elizabeth rode just behind her, while James was at her side.

The mood of the group was pleasant, for there were servants to see to her needs, guards to keep watch and enough people to converse with as they crossed the miles. Their route back to Lairig Dubh would take a more southerly route: to the tip of ancient lands of Atholl following the Tay to the loch, then west along Glen Lyon and north to Lairig Dubh. Once more following the drovers' roads, they would make good time and be off them before the great cattle drives from the north and west began.

They would not visit Dunalastair on the way back, avoiding any awkwardness about James's or his father's words on the matter of her mother. She did not know if James had revealed that she'd heard their discussion, but Lord Murray was friendlier now that their wedding was approaching and now that he would gain the support of the MacLeries as well as her dowry.

She'd spoken to James about finding a match for Elizabeth so that she would be happy staying with her and James set about the task by bringing Elizabeth into their company and even into the games of chess. Ciara had been taught by a master of the game—her mother—and could beat just about any challenger. Many nights had she spent playing, for her father believed it taught logic and strategy and felt those were good skills even for his daughter. Though her mother was the most formidable opponent, winning matches over all the MacLerie men who dared play against her, her stepfather could hold his own.

Three nights after leaving Murray lands, once their evening meal was eaten, the board was set up and Ciara challenged Elizabeth. Having watched her win over her friend several times already, James offered his assistance to Elizabeth. Though quiet while moves were being considered, the game gained attention and soon most everyone was watching and bets were placed. Tavis was there and he even smiled at several of her moves.

Though James and Elizabeth were a formidable team, she still triumphed over their combined efforts, leading to more challenges for the next several nights on the journey with the board and pieces being set up on every fair evening as soon as they finished eating.

* * *

Storms overtook them for several days. The rains slowed their travels to a crawl as the paths and roads deteriorated into muck and mired the wagons down until they surrendered to the futility of fighting it. When the sun finally mastered the clouds, she and the others were ready for some freedom from their tents and wagons or other shelters sought during the storms.

She and Elizabeth walked for a bit as their supper was prepared, with several guards following close by, until they'd stretched their legs and eased the cramps in their muscles. The food on the journey was plain but filling and eaten quickly and quietly. Then some torches were placed around one of their makeshift tables and the board brought out. Ciara laughed when she noticed some of the men beginning to place wagers even though no players had claimed the board.

'So, I wonder who will claim the board first?' she asked as they walked to it. Though many milled around it, no one sat on the stools yet.

'I tire of it,' Elizabeth said with a sigh. 'Though I like to play, it does not please me as much as it seems to you.'

'Not even when you partner with James?' she asked, watching her friend's cheeks blush in reaction.

Elizabeth began to reply, but stuttered over her words. However, they had reached the others and their attention was grabbed as they approached the table, for James delivered a challenge.

'Murray challenges MacLerie!' he called out loudly, his words echoing across the small clearing. 'Who will defend the MacLerie name?'

Ciara watched as the MacLeries huddled together, whispering and nudging, deciding on who would defend their honour in this game of skill. She remained quiet. This challenge was clearly meant to be among the men only. The MacLeries parted, declaring their champion as Tavis was pushed forwards. His willingness might be questionable, but his play revealed a determined plan to win.

Stools were brought for Ciara and Elizabeth and the game went on for some time, each move a thoughtful, strategic one. The possibility of success passed back and forth between James defending the white queen and Tavis with the red and for some time even she could not tell who would be the victor. Then, as she watched Tavis concentrate on his possible moves, she noticed the slightest tightening of his lips.

Chastising herself for staring at him did not help her take her gaze off him and she continued to watch him closely, matching that small facial expression with his moves until she understood what he was about—he was deliberately allowing James to win! If James moved the wrong piece or made himself vulnerable, Tavis countered with a move that undid it. When Tavis could have claimed several valuable pieces from James, he went for the pawns. Sitting back and taking a cup offered by a servant, she thought about why he would do such a thing.

Visions of the first training fight flashed through her mind. James, inexperienced and clearly lesser in skills and ability, fighting the quintessential Highland warrior—a man trained since his youth to fight with weapons and with his bare hands. Yet, after disarming James, Tavis was taken down by a sloppy move by the younger man.

Now watching the play before her, she noticed several mistakes and bad moves on Tavis's part, ones that would seem to be aimed at allowing James to swoop in and claim victory. Tavis was subtle, though; Ciara doubted that none but those who'd mastered the game could tell.

Tavis was throwing the game.

Chapter Twelve

Once she realised it, it was difficult not to laugh. Ciara fought against it or James's victory would be for naught. The purpose of it, she did not ken, but Tavis must have a good one to manoeuvre in such a way. Winning for him was easy, losing unlikely. Throwing a match while hiding it from those who observed was more difficult.

The control of the board switched back and forth several times before she could see the upcoming move that could defeat James. If Tavis took it, she was completely wrong about him losing on purpose. If he ignored it…

His lips twitched again, ever so slightly, and if she had not been watching so closely, she would have missed it as most others looking on did. Then he made a defensive move, allowing the one that would win the game to pass by unused. James smiled then, assured of victory, and slid his piece across to claim the red queen.

The Murrays watching shouted in glee at the outcome as James reached out his hand to Tavis. As Tavis took it, his gaze flickered over to hers and she saw the truth there. The frown that followed warned her off, but it would be more difficult than that to keep her from asking about his actions.

And she would ask.

Damn! Tavis thought as he walked from the game and towards the place in the camp where he would rest for the night. He'd bid everyone a good night's rest and turned away, but her gaze burned his back. Coward that he seemed to be when it came to Ciara, he ignored it and refused to turn around. She would ask him too many questions and he did not wish to answer them.

Or examine his reasoning too closely, either.

For, as much as he wanted to—and oh, aye, he wanted to—pound James into the ground during their training or to destroy his puny attempts at the more complex strategies of chess, he could not. Any repercussions would be felt by one person.

Ciara.

Making an enemy or opponent out of her betrothed would leave her undefended once she was no longer under MacLerie protection. Which would be very soon. James seemed to have a level head, but he would not risk Ciara's safety or future by antagonising the heir of the Murrays just because he could.

Even more, Duncan's words during their talks repeated in his head. Connor's words warned him over and over again not to be the cause of problems between the MacLeries and the Murrays, and especially not between Ciara and James. Memories of Duncan's methods of calm, dispassionate behaviour during negotiations were to be his model on this journey. And that was all well and good until it involved the lass.

Had they known the truth when they issued such words to him, each at a different time before he left Lairig Dubh, that the feelings that lay buried deep in him that would be stirred by this journey? Had they seen this happening before he did?

Tavis checked his horse and grabbed his

water skins, intent on putting some space between him and her. He would fill them in the nearby stream. Walking would feel good after sitting so long at the table. It was a task that could be left to the servants, but he preferred to see to his own preparations and needs and not rely on others to provide and perform them. Halfway down the path that led to the water, the crackling of branches behind him warned of someone following him. He let out a deep breath. Turning around was not necessary, for he could identify his pursuer without looking.

'You should be settling yourself for the night, Ciara.'

He said it aloud, not waiting on a response. The footsteps behind him paused for a few seconds, but then moved rapidly, approaching him before he reached the stream's edge.

'I would speak to you,' she said, out of breath from his quick pace.

'Nay,' he said, waving her off. 'Seek your tent. We can speak in the morn.'

It had not worked before and was not successful this time, either; the sound of her steps, crunching the leaves beneath her feet came closer and closer until he could feel the heat of her at his back. So he sidestepped and watched her stumble by him, too close to stop herself. Before she could fall, he reached out and grabbed her arm, righting her on her feet, then releasing his hold.

'Go back now,' he said. Crossing his arms over his chest, he nodded with his head back towards the camp. The torches outlining the small gathering of wagons and tents could be seen clearly in the crisp night air. He wondered how she'd got past the guards he'd posted earlier?

'I would speak—'

'Go back.'

When she crossed her arms the same as he did, Tavis knew the battle was lost. Still, he had to try.

'I pray you, return now,' he said quietly, his voice sounding as breathless as hers did.

'You lost on purpose,' she accused, not moving one bit back along the path. 'This night and when you fought.'

''Tis of no importance, Ciara. Go back now.'

Even repeating the words, whether plea or order, did no good at all, for she remained as though frozen in place. He rubbed his hands over his face and stared up at the moon above, trying to work out how to make her obey.

Would speaking plainly send her back to her tent and away from tormenting him with her every word, every smile, every frown? Facing her, he nodded once more in the direction he prayed she would go.

'To what good purpose would humiliating the young lord before his people be?' he asked. 'Other than my own needs, what good would come from defeating him now?'

She startled at his words and stared at him. 'Your own needs, Tavis?'

His body reacted as it was wont to do, his flesh rising and hardening just at the very words she spoke. And, damn, but she did not even realise the effect she could have on him! Reminding himself that she belonged to another did not help at all. So, he tamped down his wayward desires and shook his head.

'I could pummel him into the ground without much effort.' He nodded back towards the camp again. 'I could have taken his queen after five moves.'

'Five? I thought at least seven.' She smiled at his boast.

'It would have taken you seven, lass. I had him in five,' he answered her back. 'No matter,' he said, shaking his head. 'To do either of those would jeopardise what we travelled to Perth to do—confirm your betrothal.'

The intelligence and acceptance in her gaze took his breath away once more. Regardless of who had fathered her, regardless of what truths she might learn on her arrival home, she was the peacemaker's daughter at heart. She understood completely the importance and the dangers of their situation. Ciara might tease or poke, but she knew her duty and knew how this would go.

The only sign of weakness or surrender to the inevitable came as she smoothed her palms over her gown and touched something in the small pouch at her waist. He'd seen her do it dozens of times during their journey; the pouch never left her belt as much as he could remember.

'What keepsake do you carry there?' he asked. As the words escaped, Tavis thought it was a question he should not have asked. A shiver moved along his spine, warning him that the answer was not one he wanted to hear or know. But, if his misgivings showed on his face, they did not stop her from reaching in the leather sack and removing the item kept there.

A wooden horse. She cupped it in her hands,

her fingers gripping and stroking it at the same time. Small and worn though it was, he recognised it immediately as the one he'd carved all those years ago before a journey much different from this one.

A lifetime ago when his future still lay spread out before him, filled with possibilities and potential. Before he was truly a man. Before he met Saraid. Before... There was so much to regret.

'I have kept it close since you made it for me, Tavis. Whenever I feel lost or unsure, it comforts me. When I wonder about my place in the MacLeries, it reminds me,' she whispered.

Her vulnerability, the lost expression in her eyes, nearly drove him to his knees. When she let her guard down, when she let the confidence she exuded with every breath she took drop, she was dangerous to him and his resolve about his part in the life.

Tavis looked at the horse, lowering his gaze from Ciara, and remembered the exact moment when he saw her play with the small toy for the first time. Duncan had asked him to make it for her, knowing of his skill in woodworking. And knowing he had siblings almost her age, he'd asked Tavis to look after her on the jour-

ney from Dunalastair to Lairig Dubh. Neither
of them, he suspected, knew the lifelong connection that was being forged because of it. As
he held the horse carefully, knowing he could
break it if he even tightened his fist around it,
Tavis realised that he had not carved in a long
time.

Since Saraid's death.

Holy Christ! He would not survive if Ciara
continued to remind him of every weakness in
his character and the lack in his life! He turned
the carving over in his hand and realised that
she'd worn it smooth over the years until the
head had no ears and the legs had become little
stubs. A sad laugh bubbled up inside of him as
he saw the proof of her devotion to his creation.

'Hell, Ciara, 'tis worn to nearly nothing,' he
said, offering it back to her. She lifted her chin
for a moment and he noticed the way her lips
trembled. Then she took a deep breath and let it
out, an exasperated sound escaping that echoed
across the few steps that separated them. With
that, she regained control and the woman who
stared back at him was the decisive, confident
Ciara.

'I expect it will survive this journey, but not

another,' she said with a hint of sadness in her voice.

Did she speak of the wooden toy or of something else? A reference to the feelings between the two of them, mayhap? His chest ached as he understood the reality of the loss between them that was coming and he closed his fingers carefully around the toy. Anger mixed with the frustration that lived beneath his skin now and before he could think to stop the words, they escaped his mouth with no way to return them.

'I will carve another.'

The sparkle in her eyes at his offer hit him like an axe. But he knew he would do whatever she needed to keep her strong, especially since he would not, he would never be at her side again to protect her or guide her as he had so very often. A call from the camp stopped any other words or promises.

'Tavis? Is the lass with you there?' young Dougal yelled to him. They were just beginning to discover she was gone.

'Aye,' he replied. 'She is on her way back there now.'

Tavis watched as she nodded and turned back away from him. He stopped her before she took a step.

'This is still yours,' he said, handing her the first carving. Ciara opened the pouch and placed it inside, positioning the sack on her belt where she'd worn it throughout their journey.

She left without another word, but the damage was already done. He'd been trapped by a wooden animal, skewered by his own memories and desires to protect her and finished off with his own promises. Tavis walked a few paces behind her, making certain she reached the camp, then turned back towards the stream.

He ran his hands through his hair as he walked to the edge of the rushing water. Did he even remember how to carve? Did he still have the small knife he used to work on wood? How had he got himself in deeper when it was the worst thing he could do now? Tavis did not realise he was searching for a good piece to work on until he'd picked up several and tossed them aside.

Giving up on finding any measure of rest this night, he strode back to the camp, then searched his leather satchel until he found the knife. It took him some time to find the right branch of the right age, dryness and size, but he found it. Carving always eased his tension and he hoped it would again...now. But as dawn's first light crept into the skies above him, he understood it no longer worked that way.

And when he saw the rough shape of the wooden carving, Tavis grasped that he was in more trouble now than he had been when he had let Ciara see him throw the chess game to James. A horse, it was not. Held up against the brightening morn, all he could see was a heart—ragged, uneven and much like his felt this day.

Chapter Thirteen

Their journey continued and though she thought she saw Tavis working on a small piece of wood, he never showed her his work or mentioned it. With no idea of what had made her reveal the worn-down toy, she was glad she had so he understood that he did matter to her—and would continue to matter even when the toy was the only reminder of him she would have. Chess remained their evening entertainment, but she never witnessed Tavis allowing James to win again, though it was possible he'd become more skilled at hiding it.

All four of them, for Elizabeth joined in once more, partnering with James or Ciara, but never another, traded victories after that night. Ciara noticed that her friend was coming to like James, no matter her concerns over his comments about her past. They argued during their travels and during their shared meals like friends did, so Ciara was pleased. Pleased that her friend would be happy staying with her and pleased that James was taking the time to learn more about her and taking the quest for a match for Elizabeth so seriously. From the amount of time and attention he gave, Ciara was certain that he would be able to suggest possible matches when the time came.

When they reached the furthest west they would travel, it was decided they would take a day of rest before heading north into the more mountainous roads. Though they were anxious to proceed, the next part of their journey would require them to be well rested and ready to cover an arduous path. So, they set up a camp and raised tents for the women. Some of the men hunted for fresh meat for dinner while the servants prepared for it. Once a safe perimeter had been established, James invited her to walk with him. Tavis's gaze followed them; she could feel it on her, as they circled the tents and wagons.

She waited and waited for him to lure her

aside, but he did not. He spoke of her skills at
chess and riding and asked about her parents,
all the while holding her hand. Ciara wondered
at his lack of interest now in plying her with
kisses when he had seemed to enjoy it when
he had. Why she worried, she knew not, but it
bothered her in some way. When she had tried
to lean in close and give him the opportunity,
he'd neatly stepped away.

Always polite, always attentive he was, but
always maintaining a distance between them,
whether alone or with others. If she was as candid with herself as she tried to be with others,
she would have considered what she thought
the real reasons were. But she had held her
doubts and hopeless yearnings at bay each day
and waited for him to show some sign of passion for her.

The meal that night reminded her of the
ones in Broch Dubh with the laird and his
wife. Lord and Lady Murray seemed to accept her more and more with each passing day
as though she had overcome some objections
they might have had. Ciara began to believe
that she might be able to marry and be content
after all. She spent some time each day riding with James's mother and learning about

his family, their history and plans for the improvement of their lands. Regardless of their strained conversations at first meeting, Lady Murray had begun to share titbits of interesting gossip and information about their various relatives and relations.

But this evening, after the meal was finished, James asked Tavis to partner with Ciara in another game of chess while he played with Elizabeth on his side. The two men seemed to tolerate each other now that they were on the road, with Tavis instructing James in fighting techniques whenever they stopped to rest. And James took his occasional defeats at Tavis's hand in training or in play in his stride.

So, by the light of the fire and a few torches, the game began. She'd watched Tavis play many times now, both as her father's favourite opponent and several times during this journey, so she understood how he approached this game. Their styles complemented each other's—his more conservative and hers bolder—and they could read the moves to come, too. The rules set out before the game allowed each team to alternate their moves, so that Elizabeth followed Tavis while Ciara followed James. A small crowd gathered to cheer on the players, and wagers, as the men seemed wont to do, were called out also.

James and Elizabeth played well, but they were no match for Ciara and Tavis once they decided they would win. And it was a near thing, that, for at one point she would swear he was giving the game away. As their final few moves became apparent, he held back no longer and worked with Ciara to claim their opponents' queen.

Once the game was finished, Tavis returned to his men and James escorted her and Elizabeth back to their tent. Elizabeth left them alone, making her way inside while they stood outside. James stepped closer and Ciara waited for his kiss, anxious to notice any changes now that she was becoming accustomed to him and surprised yet again when he did not. With a glance at the closed flap of the tent, he bid her a good night's rest and turned to leave. Unwilling to allow the chance to pass, Ciara took his hand and pulled him closer, leaning up and touching her mouth to his. He did not step away, but this kiss was the same as the rest had been.

Nice.

Giving up on her quest to change how she

reacted to him, she whispered her farewells and entered the tent she shared with Elizabeth.

She tossed and turned that night, wondering if James had had a change of heart about accepting her as his wife. Or mayhap he was just trying to respect her before their wedding?

Confused, Ciara had lost most of last night's sleep and found that day's travel more difficult. She dozed off in the saddle and nearly fell, saved only when Tavis noticed.

'Here now, Ciara,' he said, startling her awake, 'let me adjust the strap on your saddle. It looks loose.'

Tavis guided Ciara and her mount out of the line and off into a clearing. Calling out orders for everyone to continue, he jumped down and walked to her side.

'Are you well, lass?' he asked as he checked the strap, though he could see nothing was wrong with it. 'You looked to be falling asleep and off the horse.'

She rubbed her eyes and face and shook her head. 'I did not sleep well and I am tired of travelling.'

Tavis walked around to check the other strap and to get a better look at her. She'd seemed happy on the journey, anxious even to get back to Lairig Dubh as they got closer, though he suspected it was more about speaking to her parents than anything else. The urge to comfort her was as strong as it had ever been so he stepped back.

'We should reach home by nightfall tomorrow, if we push through on the morrow,' he said. 'I plan to send a man ahead once we are on the road in the morning.' Her eyes did brighten for a moment, then they lost their shine.

He climbed back on his horse and turned to her. 'Do you worry over what they will tell you?'

'Aye,' she said quietly. 'I have never felt so unsettled in my life. I wake on the morrow as one person, but once we reach home, I may be someone else.'

He leaned over and placed his hand on hers. It was as much as he would allow himself and did it only because she wore an expression of complete devastation in her eyes as they spoke on this. 'You will never be anyone but Ciara. No one, no one's words or story, can change the person you are inside.'

'Oh, Tavis, if only I could believe it,' she

whispered to him. 'Or if I could convince myself it matters not.'

'Do you believe that your parents did this out of malice?' he asked, trying to help her focus on the important things.

'Nay, I know they did not.'

'Do you believe that any MacLerie hopes for your humiliation?'

She met his gaze then and shook her head. 'Other than my parents, I do not think anyone in Lairig Dubh really cares about what happens to me. Once I am gone, no one will even notice.'

'I care, Ciara. God forgive me, but I will know you are gone,' he admitted.

The silence spun out between them, but he would not look away from her.

'Why? Just tell me why?'

She had no idea that her words mirrored those of James when he had asked about Tavis's role in Ciara's life.

'Because I am your friend,' he said.

He purposely misunderstood and could not give her the answer she wanted, no matter how much the words pushed to be released from within him. Anger, mostly at himself, bubbled up inside him, daring him, shoving him, driving him to do the one thing he could not.

Fighting the urges roiling barely under his control, Tavis wondered if he could make the larger admission and damn himself and maybe even damn both of them. Then he realised that to speak the words he wanted to say to her would give hope where none could be. He bit his tongue rather than speak the oath that formed in his heart—*I do love you, lass.* A single tear trickled down her cheek as she waited for words that would not come.

Could not come.

'Say it, Tavis,' she begged, 'before it is too late.'

She was tearing his heart out in pieces. She had no idea what she asked of him. Not just for the words—she wanted him to act on those words and claim her. He could not tell her how he'd been responsible for Saraid's death and could not face causing hers, too. He could not share with her that he would rather watch her walk away than watch her die through his selfishness and negligence as Saraid had.

'I killed one wife, Ciara. I would rather watch you marry another than to lose you as I did her.'

She gasped at his words and paled. Her horse reared, reacting to the tension in her position, but Ciara got it under control quickly. Before they could speak further on the words he'd said and what he'd revealed, James approached and called out to them. For once he was glad of James's interruption, for it saved him from humiliating himself before her and kept him from taking a step that could lead to disaster for both of them. Tavis nodded and moved ahead of Ciara to allow James to ride next to her.

He heard the polite enquiries and Ciara's bland replies and tried not to turn back and check on her now that she'd heard part of his truth. She had been too young to know what had happened to Saraid. No matter that, for she did deserve to learn what had happened both in her own life and in his since it stood between them so firmly. But they had no more opportunity for private conversation before they arrived back in Lairig Dubh the following night as he had told her they would.

As they rode into the yard, he knew that all the pieces would fall into place in the puzzle that was their lives and she would understand all of it…

And then she would leave Lairig Dubh and him forever.

Chapter Fourteen

No one said a word as they rode into the village. Thoroughly exhausted by the hard pace of the day, they were a much different group than the one that had begun the journey with a light mood. Dust-covered and hungry, they passed through the gates and Tavis nodded to the men on duty.

As he'd told Ciara, he'd sent messengers ahead so he knew the laird and lady would be waiting in the hall, along with Duncan and Marian and, most importantly, a hot meal for all. While the wagons followed the path around to the side of the tall stone keep as he'd instructed the drivers to do, the Murray warriors stood waiting for their lord and lady to dismount—or climb from her wagon—and to be dismissed by them before following his men to the barracks. Connor and Jocelyn stood on the steps, waiting to greet their newest ally.

'Welcome to Lairig Dubh,' Connor said as he walked down the steps to greet them. 'You look a bit road-worn, so we can leave the official duties until morn,' he offered.

Tavis knew this next part, for he'd watched Connor do it many times—sometimes to make his rank clear and sometimes to put visitors at ease. This time he was not certain which purpose this was for.

'I am Douran and this is my wife Jocelyn MacCallum, Lady MacLerie.' Connor lived without the ceremony of his title as earl until or unless it suited him. This was a simple reminder that the MacLeries had reached a level within the kingdom and within the king's favour that this branch of the Murrays had not. Tavis watched as they and their son bowed to Connor, acknowledging that rank.

'May I present my son James, my lord,' Murray said, pointing to him.

The younger man did the same and waited on Connor before speaking. Ciara was greeted as the family she was and Tavis wanted to laugh and he could see the corners of Jocelyn's mouth threatening the same. Connor waited a few moments before holding his hand out in a more personal greeting.

'But we will be more than allies, William and Eleanor, and James, if I may?' Connor met their gazes. 'We will be family, so we need not stand on ceremony. Please call me Connor and my wife Jocelyn.'

It was interesting to watch as he did it, even knowing it was for effect only. The tension dissolved and Tavis followed them inside where he knew Duncan and Marian would be waiting. He could see the nervousness increasing in Ciara, for she stood rigidly now and her hands trembled. He hoped that she would get a good night's rest before tackling the serious matter with her parents.

They entered the keep and walked along the corridor until they reached the hall. Tables had been set up with food and Tavis nodded to those he passed on the way to the front of the hall. Though servant in the Murrays' hall, he had some status here and would give his report directly to Connor after the others left.

The guests were introduced to Duncan and Marian, as well as Rurik and some other of Connor's retainers and his steward, and then seated. Some informal conversation went on while the food was served and he noticed how quiet Ciara was through it all. The welcome from her parents had been a warm one and he watched as she melted into her mother's embrace. A few words were exchanged and then Ciara was seated between her parents and James.

It was a simple meal, but nourishing and filling and very satisfying after the meals on the journey. It took a short time and soon Gair, Connor's steward, escorted the Murrays to the chambers above that had been prepared for them.

Less than an hour after they reached the keep, all was quiet and Connor waited in his chambers for Tavis's report. He gave Connor time to speak to Jocelyn before climbing the steps and was surprised, though he should not have been, to find her with Connor when he entered.

'So, tell me of the Murrays and their heir,' Connor began.

He spoke about the lands, the holdings, the people and then the family, giving his personal opinion and making assessments as Connor asked questions. Then Tavis reported about the journey, both to and from Perthshire, along with his opinion of Lord and Lady Murray and James.

'So, will this be a good match as well as a good treaty?' Connor asked. Jocelyn watched him intently as he began to speak.

'They seem companionable, from what I've seen,' he admitted. 'James is not opposed to taking her as wife.'

Connor snorted. 'Certainly he is not! With what that family will gain from this, he would take my horse to wife if it was offered.'

'Connor!' Jocelyn warned with a word. Tavis forced a laugh at Connor's attempt at humour and Jocelyn gave him a dark look, too. This particular truth hurt more than others, for Ciara was simply a means to an end for the Murrays and her virtue and honour, present or missing, meant nothing to them if it brought them the wealth they needed.

Connor shrugged as though he had not said anything offensive and then asked, 'And what of Ciara? Will this match suit her?'

The silence that filled the room was deafening as they waited on his answer. It seemed to matter a great deal to the laird if she would be happy. As though he'd heard Tavis's thoughts, Connor nodded.

'She is the first of our children to be given off in marriage,' the laird explained.

Tavis understood Connor meant the first from among him and Duncan and Rurik, though his own daughter would most likely be next for a marriage arrangement, if one was not already being planned.

Tavis tried, he really did, but this time answering a question that would result in the marriage going forwards stopped him. He pushed his hair away from his face and rubbed his forehead. He just could not seem to say the words of approval this time. He'd tried convincing Ciara that the match was a good one for her and hated every word he spoke on its behalf.

'You will have to ask her that question, Connor. Only the lass knows for certain.'

Connor frowned and Jocelyn smiled and Tavis did not know which reaction he should worry over more. Knowing his words would be taken as something they were not, he tried to explain.

'Ciara knows that this is your will. That this agreement will benefit both clans. That it is her duty to accept it unless there are serious reasons not to. I think that she will do her duty.'

Now Connor smiled and Jocelyn frowned, making him more nervous.

'I will speak to Duncan in the morn after he's spoken to her.'

'She knows.'

The words hung out there between them and no explanation was needed as to what she knew.

'Did Iain tell her?'

'Nay, she overheard a conversation about her mother. She asked me to confirm it.'

'What did you tell her, Tavis?' Jocelyn asked, worry and concern threading her voice.

'I told her I did not know the whole truth of it, only that I'd heard the same rumours. 'Twas not my place, Jocelyn,' he said.

'Nay, 'twas not. We'd all hoped there would be no need. That no one would be foolish enough to speak of the past with her.'

'And no one did. The lass overheard a private talk between father and son that she was not meant to hear. James apologised to her and to me, on your behalf. He understands the seriousness of raising such insults now.'

'I do not envy Marian this night,' Jocelyn

said quietly. ''Tis a terrible thing when sins of the past rise to meet you.'

The laird and his wife both shared the same haunted expression, clearly thinking of the same matter and one that he had not been privy to all those years ago. He'd been a boy when Connor got his reputation as the Beast of the Highlands and the rumours flew about him killing his first wife. When he was of an age to serve and began under Duncan's supervision, no one said or believed such things. From the glance just exchanged, there must be some truth to that rumour to cause such pain to both of them.

'Is there anything else, Tavis?' Connor asked.

'Oh, Jocelyn, I spoke to your brother and he sends his greetings. He hopes to visit before the weather turns.'

Jocelyn smiled and Connor frowned. Athdar's initial visit here was the cause of her being forced to marry Connor, but things were more cordial between them now.

'My thanks, Tavis,' Jocelyn said, walking over to where Connor stood. 'And my thanks for carrying out this duty.'

''Twas my honour,' Tavis said. 'Connor.

Jocelyn. I will see to my duties in the morn.'
Nodding to each of them, he turned and left
the chamber.

He tried to ignore the anger that simmered
just below the surface now. He attempted to
convince himself of how good it would feel to
sleep in his own bed and wake in his own house
on the morrow. He walked swiftly through the
keep, checked on the horses and wagons, then
made his way out through the gates and down
to the village. Without clear reason or intention, he took the path that passed by Duncan's
cottage.

Though a wealthy man, Duncan and Marian
and their children lived simply, preferring a
cottage in the village now to chambers in the
keep. As he walked by, he noticed that no light
came from within. Ciara had looked ready to
drop, so he hoped she was resting before facing the troublesome conversation in the morn.
The rest of the village was quiet and dark, as
was his cottage.

He opened the door and found fresh water in
a bucket on the table, along with some food—
bread and cheese—wrapped next to it. He paid
a few coins to one of the women in the village to see to its keep when he travelled on the

laird's business and she had. Clean linens on the bed and wood and peat by the hearth were ready for his use. It was well-spent money, in his opinion, to come back to a clean, stocked house and not need to worry about such matters.

Tavis removed his garments, washed as best he could so he didn't befoul the clean sheets and fell on to the bed in exhaustion. Though he expected to lie awake and think about all that had been said and done, the next thing he knew, the sun was shining through the open shutters.

And he wondered if Ciara yet slept.

Though she had expected to spend the night dreading the morn, her body, mind and heart had been too drained to do anything but collapse into the hold of sleep. She woke as she usually did when in her own bed, with her younger brother and sister pouncing on her and begging for news. This time, their questions went on endlessly until her mother entered and intervened, ordering the young ones to give Ciara a chance to wake.

The love that shone in her mother's eyes this morn was overshadowed by fear and guilt, so Ciara knew the reckoning was close at hand.

Tempted to pull the bedcovers over her head and claim illness, she understood she was long past such antics and could not avoid, did not wish to avoid, learning the truth of her and her mother's past.

In truth, Ciara wanted answers almost as much as she dreaded getting them. She remained in bed long enough to hear her siblings being hustled out of the cottage with instructions to visit their aunt and cousins in the keep. She was debating her approach when her mother entered, carrying a steaming mug in each hand.

'Duncan did not know if you wished to speak only to me or to both of us,' she began.

From the way her mother's hands shook, Ciara worried that they would both be doused with hot liquid. She pushed back the covers, climbed from the bed and took them from her, placing them on the table near her bed.

'Should he be present? I have no idea of what to expect, so you are the better judge of it.'

'Duncan,' she said, raising her voice ever so much. Her stepfather must have stood at the ready, for he entered in only a moment.

'Good morning,' he said, walking over and kissing her on the forehead as he always did.

The tears started even then. 'Did you get any rest?'

'Aye,' she said, wiping the first of what she knew would be many tears from her eyes.

Her mother sat on the edge of her bed while she chose the chair. Duncan stood near the door in the stance she'd seen countless times before—the negotiator ready to listen and evaluate. Ciara had thought about what to ask first all the way home from Perthshire, but now, when faced with the situation, she could not form a single question. Duncan cleared his throat and nodded to her mother.

'Ciara, first I need you to understand that what is said between us here today can go no further. You cannot share what we say with anyone, not James, not even Tavis or Elizabeth. And I must have your sworn word that you will keep this all secret.'

'No one else knows?' she asked. 'The laird? Uncle Rurik?'

'They may have their suspicions and Jocelyn knows some of it, but only Duncan, my brother Iain and I know the truth that I am going to share with you.' Stunned at this disclosure, Ciara nodded.

'Nay, Ciara. We need you to speak the words

giving your sworn oath. This goes beyond a family matter, it affects a number of clans, treaties, reputations and innocent lives,' Duncan explained. 'Say the words.'

He always did that during negotiations on a treaty or agreement—both parties, all parties, needed to speak the words about what they were agreeing to so there was no question that they understood the arrangements. And it always ended with their sworn oath, spoken and written.

'Aye, Father. I swear that I will not share whatever you tell me this day with anyone. I will not speak of it with anyone, even Uncle Iain, if that is your wish?' Duncan nodded to Marian and Ciara steeled herself for what was coming.

'You heard the old rumours, then?' her mother asked. 'The ones calling me the Robertson Har...' She could not say the words, so Ciara nodded. 'They are not true, Ciara. I came to my marriage bed with Duncan a virgin, though no one could know it.'

'But you had me before you married him,' she said. 'I had five years when you...' Her mother took her hand and held it.

'Although you are my daughter in spirit and

in heart and in every way important, I did not give birth to you, sweetling.'

If Ciara thought hearing the rumours unsettled her, this sent her reeling. Her bedchamber dimmed and began to swirl before her eyes. Sucking in a deep breath, she squeezed her eyes closed and hoped the dizziness would pass.

'Ciara. Ciara!' Duncan said loudly, tapping on her cheek. She forced her eyes open and found him standing with the mug of tea in front of her face. 'Drink this.' He held it at her mouth and tipped it, so she had no choice but to take it in. Within the tea hid a good measure of whisky and she drank it down.

'Then who...?' she managed to squeak out. No matter what else the rumours said, they had never questioned that she was the daughter of Marian Robertson.

'My dearest friend and sister by marriage died giving birth to you. She placed you in my arms and begged me to protect you and care for you.'

'Beitris? Uncle Iain's wife?' she asked. 'How could that be?' There were several glances exchanged between them before her mother spoke again.

'My father was going to shame her for...'

Her mother paused and could not say whatever she'd planned to. She tried several more times, but her tears flowed heavily. She looked to Duncan now, pleading silently for him to continue since she could not.

'Beitris and Iain could not conceive a child together. They tried for years and lost at least two babes. So, in desperation, she agreed when he brought others to their bed.'

Plain, simple words that tore her world apart and destroyed every part of her being.

Ciara could usually come up with questions to clarify issues or to explain situations, but she was completely dumbfounded by this news. Her uncle could be her father. Her mother was not the woman who gave her life. No one was who she thought they were, including her. But this was only the beginning and she closed her eyes against the rest.

'The old laird, Devil take his soul, was determined to shame Beitris and to protect his heir. Marian could keep you if she would take the attention and the shame on herself. She did it for you, for her friend.' The disgust was clear in his voice. 'The old laird announced to all that while Beitris and her babe died in childbirth, Marian took men to her bed and shamed her family. He called her a whore and cast her out.' Duncan paused then and she opened her eyes to see him tightening his fists again and again. 'The word and story spread across the Highlands, hiding the real truth.'

'The only honourable thing the old bastard did was to make the arrangements he'd sworn to do and you and Marian were sent away to kin on the other side of Robertson lands.'

Her mother, nay, her aunt…nay. No matter the story. No matter the way it had happened, the woman sitting before her, torn by these admissions of the past, was her mother. And now she took a breath and spoke.

'I raised you and thanked God every day that I was blessed with you, Ciara. If I carried any shame, I knew it was not true. It was worth any cost I needed to pay to raise you when your real mother could not.'

'Is Uncle Iain…?' She could not finish the sentence now as she thought on numerous encounters with the man who might be more than he ever admitted.

'He could be,' her mother said. 'There were the others involved, but you do resemble him.'

When she calmed a bit, she noticed the terrible fear in her mother's eyes and went to her.

Her mother opened her arms as she had done countless times before and Ciara fell into them. The embrace became something more and Ciara cried in her arms for the pain and humiliation Marian had suffered to keep her safe.

'I can never thank you enough for what you did for me...for your friend...for everything,' she whispered, kissing her mother's cheek. 'Never.'

Ciara glanced over at the only father she'd known and nodded to him. He cleared his throat against the tears she could see in his eyes. 'Now you understand why this must be kept secret?' he asked.

He expected her to use her mind in this and she tried to, even though she was overwhelmed by the disclosures and the truth. Examining all those who could be harmed, she realised that this truly did affect a number of clans, the honour or dishonour of many people and the innocence of a woman who agreed to give her husband a child by any means.

'I do,' she said.

Thinking about something that Tavis had witnessed, she asked about the visit from Beitris's family some months later. 'Why did

Beitris's family come here? Tavis told me you were questioned,' she said, facing her father.

This time it was his turn to pale at her question. Again her parents glanced at each other. They were not expecting this matter to be brought up, but she needed to understand as much of the whole truth as she could discover.

'Rumours flew about the night of your birth. Some in the keep heard a bairn's cry. Others claimed to see you being spirited out of the keep alive. Worse, one of the men involved confessed his part on his deathbed and Beitris's family learned of it. Knowing that my word was my bond, they asked if your mother, Marian, came to my bed a virgin or if she could be your mother.'

Of all the things she could have heard, this was the most shocking for its implications on his honour.

'You lied for her?' she whispered, fearing that saying those words in any volume was a terrible thing. The accusation could have resulted in punishment or even a challenge if uttered by a man in public, but her surprise was so great, the words blurted out.

'You were her child. Losing you would have

destroyed her and I could not allow that to happen.'

His words were a declaration of the deepest kind of love imaginable and her heart swelled listening to it. A man of honour who would give it up for the woman he loved…and still loved just as deeply from the way he gazed at her now.

There were probably other questions, but Ciara could not think of them now. What she had heard thus far changed everything she knew about her family, her clan and herself and she would need time to come to an understanding of what this all meant. For now, she would consider everything and speak to her parents again when she'd calmed down more. If she thought to speak about it further, the loud knock on the cottage door stopped her. Duncan left her chamber, closing the door as he did, and went to see who knocked. She remembered just as his voice reached them there.

'Ah, James! Welcome! Elizabeth, come inside,' Duncan said loudly, loud enough that most of the village probably heard him.

Ciara started to go to the door, but her mother stopped her. 'Let him handle this. You need time to…'

'Stop crying and let my eyes stop swelling?' she asked quietly.

She never looked delicate or dainty or feminine when she cried. Instead her eyes swelled, her nose looked like a bulbous mess and nothing helped except time. Tavis had teased her more than once over it and she'd known it was true when she peered into the looking glass for herself. Ciara smiled sadly and nodded.

The conversation in the other room continued and her father ended up sending James off with Elizabeth for a tour of the village since Ciara was too fatigued to leave her bed this morn. When the door shut, Ciara waited several moments before leaving her chamber.

'Elizabeth seemed agreeable to showing James through the village. They hope you will feel up to the ceilidh this evening at the keep.' Elizabeth was her closest friend and she would always appreciate her help in this.

'I will.'

'James tried to apologise to me for upsetting you.'

Ciara smiled then. James was trying to be honourable about this predicament since it was his words that had revealed it to her.

'He seems genuinely sorry that I overheard it all.'

'A good sign for a young man to take responsibility for his actions, even if it was accidental,' her father said.

'So you approve of this match, then?' she asked. Looking from one to the other, she could see they differed in opinions in this.

'Aye, I do, Ciara,' he said plainly. 'This just confirms it for me.' Her mother snorted— snorted!—but looked away when she turned to her.

'Mother?' Ciara said, giving her the chance to voice her concerns. An unspoken but communicated thought passed from one to the other and her mother simply shrugged, keeping silent about any concerns she might have.

'This is your decision to make, sweetling. I will support you in it.'

They turned to leave, with a suggestion that she rest, when she remembered the other question that nagged at her mind and memory.

'My dowry,' she said. They stopped and faced her, this time with their hands joined. 'Is it from him?'

'Iain?' her father asked.

'Aye.'

He shook his head in reply. 'He provided a dowry for both you and Marian. We decided to put it together for you, since your sister, our Beitris, inherits lands from her Robertson grandmother.'

''Tis blood money, then, paid for his part in his wife's, my mother's, death?'

'I think of it as repayment for all that was lost, Ciara. We existed in poor circumstances when both of us were entitled to more, much more, but could not claim it.'

'To ease his guilty conscience, then,' she offered.

'To offer help when he could not in the past,' her mother countered.

'You seem eager to forgive him for his sins, Mother.'

'Ciara, do not let this make you bitter. You were raised in love by us, given every privilege and comfort you needed. I would have refused it at the time, but decided you deserved it, to ensure a happy future.'

The irony that struck her was that the dowry was the heart of the problem for her. It made her more appealing as a bride to any and all clans who had an unmarried heir and need for gold. Without it, she might have been able to marry someone here, someone…

Ciara shook her head, trying not to allow that thought to complete itself. If she were honest, she would admit that it also gave her a measure of control that other heiresses did not have. And she did not feel like being generous in her consideration of Iain Robertson's actions in the past right at this moment.

'I understand,' she said, accepting that she would not win this argument.

They kissed her once more and then began to leave.

'I would like to walk a bit and settle this in my mind.'

'I will have a bath ready for you when you get back, Ciara. Once you feel refreshed, things will be clearer to you,' her mother said. She watched as her mother took her father's hand and met her gaze. 'We are here any time you have questions. We will answer what we can.'

She nodded and closed the door to her chamber. Finding a clean gown in her trunk, she dressed and put on her leather boots. It was a warm day out, so she needed no cloak now. She would walk to the stream and freshen her face before returning. It would give her time to

think about all these matters and the changes
wrought by them in her life. She waited for her
father to return to his duties before going outside and heading to the path next to the cottage.

And found Tavis watching her.

Chapter Fifteen

He'd been there for some time and watched Duncan arrive, James and Elizabeth arrive and leave and then Duncan depart, too. Only then did Ciara open the door and step outside. She looked terrible and calm at the same time. As she lifted her eyes and noticed him, he waited for her to turn away.

Instead, she offered him a soft smile and a nod.

'James and Elizabeth headed through the village to the keep,' he said.

'Then we should go in this direction,' she said. If her attitude should have shocked him, it did not.

He followed her into the forest and the path that led to the stream that fed the wells hereabout. They walked in companionable silence, through the hills, until they reached the banks of it. Ciara walked to the edge and knelt down, dipping her hands in the water and splashing it on her face.

'You just do not cry well, do you, lass?' he asked, already seeing proof of the answer in her swollen eyes and puffy nose and mouth. He handed her a small square of linen he'd brought along, suspecting she might need one.

'Nay, Tavis,' she said, accepting it. ''Tis one thing I do not seem to outgrow.'

He waited for her to use it and apply cold to her face before speaking to her. He wanted to ask her so many questions, but he sensed that right now she needed the silence he could give her, or she would have followed James and Elizabeth in the opposite direction. When she stopped dabbing the wet linen on her face, he knelt next to her.

'Are you well, then?'

'I think so, Tavis,' she answered, though her gaze showed no certainty.

'Did you get the answers to your questions?'

She took in a deep breath and he thought she might begin crying again. But she did not.

'I did.' She nodded and looked away from

him then, staring into the rippling surface of the stream.

'Did it change how Duncan and Marian feel about you or you about them?' He would not probe further if she did not wish to speak of it.

'I think I love them more now than I did before we talked this morn,' she said. 'Far from being unwanted, I was most wanted.'

''Tis well, then,' he said.

'Will you be at the ceilidh this evening?' Ciara stood and waited for him.

He climbed to his feet and shook his head. 'I have other duties to see to,' he lied.

'Do you, then?' He sensed she knew it for the lie it was, but did she have to challenge it?

'Ciara, please,' he whispered as she stepped nearer to him, though he could not say if he wanted her to stop or to move closer. Hell, he wanted her closer.

She stopped and stepped away and he wished she had not in the same moment he thanked God above that she had. He could not resist her when she was vulnerable and though she had stopped crying and looked considerably better than when he'd found her, he could feel her need for his support in his heart and soul.

'Forgive me, Tavis, for putting you in this

difficult position. I am still undone by what I have learned and need some time to consider the consequences of it all.'

The thing he could not ignore was that she had followed him and not James. She spoke to him about this matter and not James. Damn it all to hell! Why did she not share such confidences with her betrothed or seek him out for comfort?

Tavis knew why. He knew, he felt, the connection between them—one born in childhood fancy, nurtured through friendship and exposed during this transition into adulthood. He'd ridiculed it. He'd doubted it. He'd resisted it. He'd even tried to deny it before he was forced to accept it as real.

Through their journey, he understood it and the challenges that loving her placed in his life and hers. They each had their responsibilities to the clan and their duty was clear: she would marry James and he would leave. This love just made it more difficult.

The admission he'd just made to himself should have chilled him to his soul; however, denying it any longer was simply not within his power to do. But acting on it was something he would not do.

'Your life has thrown you this way and that for months now and especially these last weeks, Ciara. Give yourself time.'

A sad smile barely lifted the corners of her mouth. She nodded her head without meeting his gaze. 'With the harvest approaching and the cattle to be moved and all the tasks of autumn, they want the wedding to be in a week.'

No time at all and he would lose her forever.

But he would lose her sooner if he revealed the whole of the reason he feared trying to claim her. In truth, he did not fear being cast out. He could live on his own, even move to a distant cousin's village in the south, if need be. He did not fear losing everything here: his house, his duties, his friends. He would lose them soon when he moved out of Lairig Dubh for another of Connor's holdings.

What he feared most was seeing the disappointment in her eyes and watching her love for him die even as he watched Saraid die because of his foolishness.

'Would it be easier for you if I left Lairig Dubh now?' he offered. It seemed kinder than constantly be faced with a love that could not be.

'Nay,' she said, reaching out and laying her

hand on his arm. 'I pray you not to do that.' She swallowed several times and then spoke in a tear-thickened voice. 'It helps me to remember how to carry out my duty to those I love when I can see you doing the same thing.'

He nodded and stepped back, allowing her hand to drop from his arm. 'Only if you say so.'

'Come now,' she said, stepping away from the edge. 'My mother is waiting a bath for me and will seek me out if I do not return.'

He did not take her arm. 'I will see you at the ceilidh.'

That was his compromise and the only one he was willing to make. There would be count-less other people there to distract him from her. He could do it for her.

Ciara left without another word and Tavis followed her far enough to make certain she returned safely to her parents' cottage.

Then he spent the day completing tasks left undone when he had decided to accompany her to Perthshire those weeks ago. He kept so busy that he almost did not dwell on the com-ing wedding.

Almost.

Instead he took out his anger and frustra-tion in a time-proven manner that was guaranteed to wring it free from him—he challenged Rurik to a fight. Hours later, he was too weakened and battered to worry about most anything.

He barely made it to the ceilidh after all.

James sat at the high table and watched Ciara dancing with her family below. Her lithe figure moved gracefully through the steps of the dance being played on pipes, drum and harp. He smiled, knowing she would be his in a few short days. He made himself smile whenever anyone mentioned the coming wedding. It was what was expected of him now.

They would accommodate each other in their marriage, that much he had learned about her during their trip back. She'd sworn that she would come to his bed a virgin and he believed her, but that did not mean she would not be thinking of another man in her heart. James glanced across the huge hall, four or five times the size of theirs, and found that man.

Tavis MacLerie.

The laird's man. Honourable. Trustworthy. Dependable.

Yet none of those qualities had stopped him from falling in love with Ciara. Truth be told,

James could understand it, for she was a fetching lass. Intelligent. Skilled in numbers and languages. Trained by the best, her stepfather, to understand financial matters. A gift to the man who would marry her.

Though he masked it well when he knew others were watching and he would never admit it to a stranger like him, James knew Tavis loved her as James himself should.

But, he did not. Not yet and mayhap not ever.

Elizabeth returned to her chair then and he watched her long, curly dark hair sway across her back and hips as she leaned over to speak to the MacLerie before sitting down.

While Ciara intimidated him, Elizabeth did not. She smiled and took a sip from her goblet of watered wine. Turning back to watch the dancing so he did not stare at the way her lips touched the edge of that cup, he nodded towards Ciara.

'She seems well now,' he observed.

'Oh, James. She does not blame you for revealing the terrible rumours to her.' She caressed his arm in a soothing way, rubbing along his sleeve until their bare skin touched. They both moved back quickly as though it had not happened.

He knew they needed to change their topic, so he moved to one brought up by Ciara herself. An unpleasant one, but one he could draw her out with.

'Ciara has asked my help in finding a husband for you. Why do you not tell me what you favour in a man and I will think on who in my family might do well by you?'

As she leaned in and mentioned characteristics and skills she found pleasing in a man, he reminded himself it was all simply flirting. That he would marry Ciara and any feelings for her best friend would go no further. But by the time she had described her perfect man and it sounded too much like him, James knew he had a problem. Then, as she pointed out men at this celebration whose physical traits were identical to his, he reminded himself of all the reasons he must marry Ciara.

In the end, he imagined he must be as miserable approaching this wedding as Ciara was, but wondered how she never let it show.

She returned to him and spoke with both him and Elizabeth of the wedding plans. She went and brought him food and filled his cup when it emptied. Ciara was the perfect hostess as she would be the perfect wife; he had no doubt of that. And if her gaze slid over the crowd from time to time and watched Tavis through that evening, did it bother him? Strangely, it did not.

He liked the man, for even when he questioned his actions and behaviour with Ciara, the man had been frank and direct and did not deny their friendship. And once they left to return to his home and Ciara took over her duties as his wife, Tavis would be only a memory to her.

James would be the only man in her bed, he knew that, but not in her heart.

He wished it was not true. He wished he did not need to force her into this marriage and take her from the life she so clearly loved here. He wished that the dowry did not matter.

But it did and it mattered so much it pushed those other regrets out of the realm of possibilities.

And what would happen when James found a woman he wanted to love? He glanced over at Elizabeth and met her gaze as she smiled at him. Then all three of them would be trapped in the same hell until one of them died and could claim their real love.

James pulled himself from his melancholy thoughts and asked her, Ciara, to dance. She did not hesitate and he enjoyed touching her and guiding her through the pattern of the dance across the floor. For a moment, the music faded into the background and he stared deeply into her eyes, seeking some indication of her feelings for him.

And, though he saw many things there, he did not find love.

Ciara accepted his invitation, she accepted his touch and encouraged it even as they swirled around through the other couples. She wanted to enjoy James. She wanted him to enjoy her. But something was missing between them.

They drew to a stop and she introduced him to more of the MacLerie clan who joined in the feast to celebrate their coming wedding. In a week, she would join with him and become his. She would live with him, sleep with him and, if God was willing, make bairns with him. Her life would be his to control, to command and to guide. One day he would lead his clan and she would be at his side, as Jocelyn stood by Connor and even her mother stood by her father in his duties.

And she would try every day with every

breath to never let him know that she loved another.

She stumbled then, but he caught her, setting her to rights and keeping his hand on her waist until they walked back to the high table and sat. The night was nearly over when he leaned in close and whispered to her.

'I would speak to you in private, Ciara.'

She smiled. Was he finally going to kiss her again? She'd nearly given up hope of finding out if his kiss appealed to her before the wedding. 'Of course, James.'

'On the morrow?' he asked.

'Elizabeth? When did my mother say the dressmaker was coming to fit our dresses?' she asked. Elizabeth was more organised when it came to things like this.

'Mid-day. After the noon meal, but before the heat of the day reaches its peak.'

'Would you like to walk after Mass in the morning? Father Micheil will say it on the morrow and we could walk back together?'

'I will meet you there, then.'

'Jamie, he will begin just past first light,' Elizabeth said.

The familiar form of his name coming from her friend startled her. They looked at each other and then away, so Ciara did not know what to think of it. She'd never called him by anything but his whole name. He stood then, preventing her from asking about it.

'I will bid you goodnight, Ciara,' he said, lifting her hand to his lips and kissing it gently. 'Elizabeth,' he said with a nod to her friend.

Ciara watched him leave and then caught a glimpse of Elizabeth watching him, too. A strange shiver crept down her spine, but it disappeared quickly.

'Ciara. Elizabeth,' her father called their names. 'Are you ready to return home?' He and her mother stood then and bid goodnight to the laird.

'Aye,' she said. She doubted that one night of rest had replenished her and she looked forward to her bed.

She walked over to the laird and lady and thanked them for their hospitality of the evening's dinner. Since it was their custom to be the last in their hall, she knew it was fine to leave before them. A busy day would find her up and out early on the morrow, now adding a private talk with James into the many tasks she had to complete in preparation for their wedding.

They walked along the path to Elizabeth's cottage to see her home first, then on to theirs. Since the wee ones would be asleep, they trod quietly through the main room and to their chambers. Soon, the house was as silent as the entire village and Ciara found herself following an endless trail of questions and suspicions about what James wanted to talk about in the morning.

With the arrangements set and the marriage ceremony happening in a few scant days, it was most likely about that and about plans to return to his, their, home in Perthshire. There would be much to see to once her dowry was in his father's control and much for her father to oversee for the MacLeries until Connor appointed someone to handle the agreements with the Murrays.

Prime came early and Father Micheil would begin promptly, noticing anyone who arrived late. Though he would peer at them with a frown, he would never reprimand. He had performed her parents' wedding and would say hers now and it made her glad. Realising that she'd not met the Murrays' priest while there, she would ask James about that in the morning, too.

If morning ever came.

Chapter Sixteen

Marian stood next to Jocelyn during the Mass, watching Ciara and James. He touched her hand several times during prayers and Ciara smiled at him several other times. All seemed as it should between a young man and woman about to marry—respectful, attentive, even affectionate.

And it broke her heart.

Jocelyn noticed her expression and mouthed, *Is aught wrong?* to her. Marian shook her head and turned her attention back to the altar and Father Micheil's prayers. James had asked to walk with Ciara, alone, after Mass, so he wanted to speak to her on some private matter. Again, expected between a betrothed couple.

If she could only be a bird in the trees along their path!

* * *

Soon Mass was ended and she waited as Jocelyn spoke to the priest for a few moments. Ciara kissed her and squeezed her hands as she and James left and it brought tears to her eyes. She and Duncan had had misgivings and fears about sharing the complete truth with Ciara, but it was her due. They had no doubt she would hold it all in confidence, but she needed to know.

Marian had watched as Ciara realised she was not her true mother and feared that Ciara would never forgive her for the deception. Instead, after hearing their explanation, she called her *Mother* and held her as she always had, easing Marian's heartache. When she called Duncan *Father,* even after all the disclosures made to her, it made her heart swell with pride and love for the daughter who could not be more her own.

Jocelyn wrapped her arms around hers and they walked from the chapel together. Marian knew her friend's intent and it came as soon as they were away from anyone who could overhear their conversation.

'So, you told her?'

'We did.'

'She seems more at peace than I expected from such revelations,' Jocelyn observed.

She'd been the only one to whom she had told some of the truth those long years ago when she'd first arrived in Lairig Dubh with Duncan. Assisting Jocelyn at Sheena's birth had brought back the memories of that night with Beitris and Marian had suffered from them terribly. Jocelyn's friendship and her wonderful herbal tea had eased the way through one of her darkest nights.

'Ciara had heard, or overheard, many of the rumours from James and his father. At least she knows the truth about those now.'

'How did she react about her mother?' Marian remembered the desolate expression that Ciara's eye bore in those moments, but also the love she saw there for her, too.

'As we expected. It shocked her to her soul,' Marian admitted. 'But then she accepted it. She asked about her true father.'

'Did you tell her?'

'Aye,' she replied, keeping some of this particular truth to herself, for no one save Duncan and Iain knew about that situation and Iain's secret life. Jocelyn believed her brother Ciara's father and never spoke of it.

They were near the place on the path where it split, part going uphill to the keep, the other going downhill into the village. Their duties called them in different directions for the moment, though Marian would see to James's parents later. For now, the laird was acting host to his newest ally and discussing all manner and sort of business with him, much to the Murray's delight when she'd observed some of the exchanges.

She took hold of Jocelyn's hand before they parted.

'I have been turning this over and over in my mind and cannot come up with a reason why Tavis would not marry Ciara. The wealth would be one matter, if Tavis cared about such things. Her education might be another, for it intimidates most men when they discover her abilities. But there must be something more personal to keep his heart locked away from her.'

'Saraid?' Jocelyn asked.

'It must be. I did not know her well, Jocelyn. Did you?'

'Nay.' Jocelyn shook her head. 'Her family moved here just before their wedding. Tavis met her while travelling with Connor to the southern holding.'

'The only person who could answer questions about her is Tavis,' Marian added. 'And Ciara, for she worshipped him in those days and she followed them everywhere.'

'The only two people to whom we cannot speak without raising questions.' Jocelyn sighed. 'It seems that Ciara will marry James, then. Which—' she touched Marian's arm '—does not appear to be a bad match after all.'

Marian crossed her arms over her chest and rubbed them, staring at the path the two had taken for their walk. 'Nay, it is not a bad match. It will just take her so far from here and to a man who does not love her. But that is not a bad match.'

Jocelyn met her gaze. 'And how is that different from our marriages? I came here believing that Connor would murder me the way he murdered his first wife. You came here, forced to marry a man who knew you'd deceived him and everyone else.'

Marian laughed. 'Only Rurik and Margriet's match must have been less trying.'

'Do not be so certain of that. Our Rurik with the way he loves women and a woman who grew up in a convent? I am certain there were some rocks on that path.'

It did calm her worries when she thought of it that way. At least James and Ciara liked each other at the beginning of their marriage. Love could grow later.

It could.

James took her hand as they walked from the church and she decided to focus on all the things she liked about him as they strolled in the privacy of the forest for this 'talk'.

She liked the way he entwined their fingers as he held her hand. She liked the way he did not seem threatened by her behaviour and encouraged her opinion on matters at hand. She liked the sound of his voice as he spoke.

There. All good things on which to build.

They stopped and he pulled her into his arms, tilted down and kissed her without any warning. He glided his lips over hers, pressing until she opened—as Tavis had—and then moved his tongue into her mouth. Trying to participate more, remembering his comment about her previous one, she slid her arms around his neck and pressed her body against his, the way it had done on its own during the kisses with Tavis.

James seemed to like it, wrapping his arm around her waist and holding her close. But his mouth just remained there, not doing anything that engendered those hot passions to run in her blood.

Just when she thought he would bring it to an end, he slid his other hand up and skimmed over her breast. Once he found it, he cupped her, rubbing there several times. He lifted his head then and whispered to her, 'You are an innocent.'

Ciara knew the touch was scandalous, one that should not be permitted before their marriage bed, but it did not feel scandalous to her. It did not urge her to want more. It did not heat her blood as a simple kiss from Tavis did.

'Is that a bad thing, then?' she asked.

'Nay! A man likes to know he will be the first with his wife,' James explained. He stepped back and stared at her. 'If I might use some of that candour of yours?' She nodded. 'From what I'd been told, about those rumours...' he hesitated for a moment before pushing on '...I did not expect a virgin bride and had accommodated myself to that notion.'

Ciara blinked at him several times as she listened. 'And you were willing to accept that?'

'Aye, for the many reasons that we both know about, I would have.' James looked at her. 'There was one that gave me some hope. All the stories spoke of your mother's past; none of that behaviour ever was rumoured after she married Duncan. So, if your mother could be faithful, I expect that you can, too.'

Stunned by these revelations, she just shook her head and laughed, now knowing the truth of her mother's 'past'. He'd considered her less than virtuous and was willing to accept her.

That damned dowry! Founded on nothing less than blood money and determined to shape her life and marriage.

'Did you like that?' he asked, glancing at her breast.

'Aye, it was nice,' she answered. It did not stir her to excess or make her want to lie down with him, but mayhap it would if there was more? 'Would you…?' She glanced down and then met his gaze.

James stepped in close and kissed her mouth again. He held her close and then began kissing a path down her cheek and neck. That felt nice, too. Then he turned her slightly and placed his hand on her again, this time with more pressure and rubbing his thumb over its tip. Nice.

He was just about to kiss her mouth again when some branches and leaves crackled, alerting them that they were not alone. They lifted their heads and found Elizabeth there. Jumping back and pushing her hair away from her face, she smiled at her friend. A bit embarrassed by being discovered during such a personal moment, she was surprised by Elizabeth's glare.

'My pardon, Ciara and James,' she said, not even looking at him. 'The dressmaker is coming before this morn, so I thought I would let you know.'

'I will be right along, Elizabeth,' she said, smiling back.

Elizabeth seemed to want to say something else, but did not. With only a nod, she turned and left. James watched her go and then turned back to Ciara.

'I suppose it was better that she found us than your parents.'

Ciara shook her head. 'Certain leniencies are permitted between betrothed couples, James. I doubt my parents think that we have not shared some intimacies by now.'

He took her hand and kissed it, beginning

to follow the path once more. She guessed that his attempts at intimacies were over.

'Believe it or not, that was not why I wanted you alone, Ciara.' He winked at her then. She liked his wink. 'I wanted to ask you something before we stand before the priest. I do not like surprises.'

'Oh? What do you wish to know?' Ciara tried to think about the wedding ceremony, but she had not witnessed one yet. She'd avoided Tavis and Saraid's those years ago and did not know all the words and prayers that would be said over and for them.

He stopped them once more and turned to face her, his blue eyes growing darker in that moment with an intensity she did not usually see there.

'Do you have or know of any reasons why we should not marry?'

Of all the things she'd thought he'd ask, that was not one of them. Did loving another man count in his opinion?

'I do not mean reasons about clans or allies or treaties, Ciara. I mean from you to me—are you content with this marriage between us?'

'Content?' What a strange word to choose. 'Is that what you seek, then? Contentment?'

He turned from her then and took a breath. Shaking his head, he spoke. 'Aye. I am not a man ruled by passions and do not seek a marriage caught up in the drama of those emotions. I am not a man of great courage. Our life in Perthshire will be very different from this Highland life you have lived here. I but seek your contentment in being my wife at my side.' He looked at her then. 'I have seen marriage ruled by passion—I have seen it before and do not wish it.'

She'd seen those marriages, too. Her parents. The laird and lady. Cousin Rurik and Margriet. All passion-filled marriages that were mostly about love. And she wanted that, too. But, clearly, and to his credit, that would not be theirs. He was not asking for her love, he was asking her to be content without it.

'So, is there any reason you do not wish to stand before the priest two days hence and pledge our vows?'

A life of contentedness spread out before her. She looked into his eyes and found more emotions there than she'd ever seen in his gaze. And there, deep within, she thought he might be asking her for a way out of this, knowing she'd backed out of other betrothals before his.

Or mayhap he simply did not want to be humiliated on his wedding day to be at the church with no bride at his side? He said he did not like drama, and that would be the worst kind of it.

Still, she had promised, even knowing that she would leave behind the passion and the love she could have, she knew she could have, with Tavis. He was so scarred by what had happened with Saraid that he could not claim what could be between them.

So.

'There is no reason, James.'

He let out his breath and looked away and in that moment she did not know if he was relieved or disappointed. Strange.

James nodded and smiled then and took her hand once more.

'Come then, your mother and Elizabeth and the dressmaker will be waiting for you.'

Although they spoke on the way back to her home, it was of nothings: the path, the weather, the ceilidh the night before. Nothing that mattered. Ciara knew that this would most likely be the pattern of their life.

They reached her cottage and found her mother and Elizabeth waiting, drinking tea with Dolina, who was making the gown she would wear for the wedding. Ciara noticed that Elizabeth's gaze went right to James's.

'Well, this is a place a man does not need to be,' James said, smiling. 'I will leave you all to your task, then.'

He bowed his head to them and took his leave.

Dolina had made the gown patterned on her others, so it would simply need a few tucks and stitches to make it fit well. They went into her chambers and Ciara removed the gown she wore and slid the new one over her head. It was made of a lovely rose-colored over-gown that would be worn over a linen chemise. More lowland than Highland in style, her mother had thought it suitable for the wedding.

'So, how was your *talk*?' her mother asked, winking at her. 'Elizabeth said she came upon you in the forest on her way here and you were *talking*.'

She laughed, knowing it would be expected. Glancing at Elizabeth and thinking of the lie she'd told, she said, 'It was a nice talk.'

'Nice is good,' Elizabeth said, reaching for another pin for Dolina.

Elizabeth liked nice. She did not like overwhelming and passionate kisses and did not seek a marriage where she would be more than content. She met her friend's gaze, then Elizabeth turned away after a moment.

'Yes, it is.'

They worked quietly then, gathering here, letting out there, until Dolina and her mother were pleased. Dolina would finish the dress and have it back here on the morn of her wedding.

The rest of the day went quickly, as the hours before her wedding seemed to go by. Ciara spent some of the time with James's mother while James worked with the men in the training yard. Unwilling to see Tavis just then, she avoided it while turning another plan over in her mind. Certain it would not work, certain he would refuse, she knew she had to try it.

Passion would not be enough. When men feared something, something they could not admit or face, sometimes it was up to a woman to show it to them. And Tavis had carried fear in his heart every day since Saraid's death. The fear had such a tight grip on him that he needed someone to help rid it from him.

She sought out the midwife who Saraid

had seen during her carrying and asked questions that had plagued her since her death. If Gunna thought her questions strange or out of place, she did not say. Most likely she thought them natural ones for a young woman about to marry and her last words, trying to ease her fears of the marriage bed and bearing bairns, confirmed it.

Just as her explanation had confirmed the one thing that still held terror over Tavis—that he or something he did or did not do caused Saraid's death.

If she did nothing else before she left Lairig Dubh as James Murray's wife, she would free her first and dearest friend from the tyranny that held his heart prisoner.

If she did nothing else before she said the words that would make her James Murray's wife, she would have the passion that she was forfeiting on the day of her marriage.

If she did nothing else before ending her time as Marian and Duncan's daughter, she would be the bold, confident woman they had raised her to be.

With a plan in mind to fulfill those needs and desires, Ciara waited for her parents and siblings to seek their rest. Once the house had settled and only the sound of night birds broke the stillness of the silence around them, she considered her plans one last time.

What she planned to do was scandalous. She had told James she would come to him a virgin, but now would offer that to Tavis. If he accepted it. And now, in the quiet of the night, she did not know if he would reject her once more.

Shaking her head, she crept from her bed and gathered what she needed. She would not let doubt or fear or guilt rule her as it did Tavis. If she would live by duty for the rest of her life, this night would be about love.

And if this was the only night she would have with him, so be it.

But she had waited almost her whole life for him and she, they, would have this night.

Chapter Seventeen

Tavis worked as hard and as long and as late as he could, trying to avoid returning to his empty cottage. He took on all opponents in the training yard and faced off with an equal number of MacLeries as well as several more of the Murrays before having enough. Aching from working out the frustration that would not be tamed, he accepted an invitation to share the evening meal with Rurik and Margriet and stayed longer than he should, speaking about another assignment from Connor.

When, with another not-subtle pointed glance at both his bedchamber's door and the door of the cottage, Rurik told him to leave, Tavis did so, walking slowly along the path back to his cottage. He was in no rush to face the empty cottage that mocked him, reminding him of promises broken and lives lost.

Strange. When he looked at the door of it, he could still see Ciara as she stood there that night, asking him to marry her. Not Saraid, whose ghost still haunted the rooms within it.

Tavis noticed that the shutters were closed. That was not how he'd left them. As he approached, he saw the flickering light of flames in the hearth through the crack between the door and the frame.

Someone had been here while he was not. Someone might yet be inside. His hand grasped the hilt of his dagger before he thought it and he positioned his body to the side of the doorway as he lifted the latch and entered carefully.

Ciara sat before the hearth, reading by the light of several candles. Her hair, loose and lovely, flowed over her shoulders. Dressed in a simple gown with a plaid shawl, she was the essence of Highland lass. His mouth watered, his hands itched and his heart ached just looking at her and knowing she could not be his.

'Ciara?' he asked, stepping further inside and sliding the dagger back in its scabbard. 'What are you doing here?'

'Waiting for you,' she said, closing the book

and placing it on the wooden mantel above the hearth. 'I needed to see you in private to speak to you.' He did not reply immediately. He waited for what seemed an eternity of time before speaking. So many wrong things to say and very few right ones crossed his mind.

'Ciara, 'tis best if we do not. The last time…' He thought about their last encounter alone in the night and how it ended up with her in his arms devouring her mouth with a kiss he could still remember and taste.

'I have a last request for my closest friend before I set off to my marriage.'

Did she have to remind him that she would leave him forever? For a brief moment when he entered the cottage, he'd allowed himself to imagine that this was how he would find her on his return each night. Waiting for him. Waiting for his touch, his kiss, his body…his love.

The words brought him back to the reality that would be—she was not his. He swallowed several times, trying to clear his throat from the sudden emotion clogging it.

'What is your request?'

'James and I spoke about our marriage and it is clear he wants a calm, sensible relationship, built on polite conversations and companionable peace.'

Tavis could believe both that she could have spoken to the man about that and that young James would be a calm, dispassionate, courteous husband to Ciara. Not that that was the way he would have her to wife, but...

A sudden vision of them in bed, with him buried deep in her flesh, urging her with hands and body to explode in passion with him. Her hair spread around them as his hands pleasured her lovely, rose-tipped breasts. He was hard before he finished the thought.

'If I must face a life of calm and sensible affection,' she said, now walking towards him, 'then I wish to know the passion and pleasure I will be missing with you.'

Bloody hell! Did she not know the temptation she was to him? How much of a struggle it had been to keep his hands to himself and to seek his own release when the need for her tempted him in the deep of the night, every night, since he'd given in and tasted her mouth?

'Ciara, I beg you to leave now,' he forced out from behind clenched teeth. 'Before it is too late.'

'It has been too late for some time, Tavis.'

She reached up and touched his cheek. 'But I will leave if you can kiss me once and let me go.' Her smile filled with wicked temptation.

Sweet Christ, but the lass knew how to challenge his resolve!

'One true kiss, Tavis. I beg you,' she whispered, the very word and the image sending blood pumping harder through his veins. 'One true kiss and I will leave with that memory in my heart forever.'

Surely he had enough honour and strength to suffer through a kiss, only one kiss before he would send her away?

He nodded.

With his hands placed firmly at his sides, he would not touch her. If he did that, he was certain that he could control himself, but damn the lass, she had other plans. When he leaned his face down to touch her lips, she placed her fingers there and shook her head.

'Nay. One kiss. I decide when.'

He was going to die and go to hell, of that he was now certain, but he had resisted her thus far and he would keep his control. He would... he must...

He might have had a chance *if* she had not reached for the belt holding his plaid in place.

If she had not moved around him, stripping him of his weapons, his belt, the plaid and the shirt under it. He could have *if* she'd not brought over a bucket of steaming water and begun to wash him.

Oh, hell, he never stood a chance and she knew it from the unrepentant gleam in her eyes.

If she was startled to find him as he was, she did not mention it. Worse, her tongue slipped out and touched her lips as she washed him.

'I have seen you before,' she whispered as she stroked the warm, wet cloth over his back and lower. 'At the stream in Dunalastair. You were naked there and I watched.'

Her words undid him and his resolve. He laughed at her admission.

'You were wicked to do that.' She laughed softly but did not stop her ministrations. 'And even more wicked to do this.'

She finished his back and drifted around front again. The virgin that she was showed herself for a moment when she reached for him and then stopped. Tavis took her hand and the cloth and wrapped them around the length of him. The expression on her face and the way she opened her mouth, breathing through it quickly, just enhanced his response and his flesh surged in her grasp. He guided her lower and then tossed the cloth aside and splashed some water over his skin to rinse the soap away as she watched.

It was time to show her that one kiss would not be enough, never be enough, but she stopped him once more by moving away.

Her hands loosened the laces behind her with practised ease. She pulled the gown over her head, giving him a clear view of her naked body beneath the sheer chemise. The flames from the hearth revealed her exquisite curves and the dark triangle of hair hiding the place he longed most to touch…and stroke…and taste. Her nipples tightened—did she even notice?—as he watched her. And as she watched him.

Bold as he knew her to be and braver than he could ever hope to be, she walked to him now and offered herself to him. Oh, aye, he would pleasure her, but he would not cross the line to dishonour another man's betrothed, idiot that the man was or not and idiot that he himself might be.

'I will not take that which is not mine,' he whispered. 'But I will give you the pleasure you seek, the pleasure that can be between a man and a woman.'

'The pleasure that can be between you and me, Tavis.'

Innocent and a seductress in every breath, she probably did not realise that pleasure did not mean he had to take her maidenhead. 'That kiss, Ciara. 'Tis time for your kiss.'

He thought her game was over, but she took off the chemise and placed her hands beneath her breasts, offering them to him. Arching her back to lift them higher, she whispered, 'Kiss me here, Tavis.'

He stared, oh, aye, he did, for this was the vision from his dreams come to life. Her lithe body, her breasts that would fit perfectly in his hands as he kissed them—all of it was straight from his dreams.

He closed his eyes and prayed for the strength to keep his honourable pledge even as he leaned down to take the tip of one of her breasts in his mouth. She gasped and he knew she'd expected a polite kiss and not the hunger-filled taking he gave. When he felt her legs tremble, he scooped her up in his arms and carried her to his bed.

He would show her the full measure of a kiss now. Kneeling next to her, he touched her with only his mouth. First he took the other nipple in his mouth and suckled it, rubbing and teasing the tip of it even harder. If he was, she would be, too. Her body arched beneath his mouth and she whispered his name over and over. Kissing and licking his way up her body, Tavis took her mouth next.

He smiled as she opened it for him, but he teased her lips, kissing them gently until she smiled. Then he possessed her there, his tongue tasting hers and then feeling the shards of pleasure shoot through him as she sucked his. Bold lass that she was, he felt her hands in his hair, pulling him closer, holding him, not letting him move away.

And that was fine with him, for he could kiss her for hours and not tire of it. He could tell from her restless, innocent movements that she did not know what pleasure still awaited her.

This had not been part of her plan at all. She'd thought, when she had been able to think, that he would hold her and kiss her. Once he declared that he would not take her virginity, she thought she understood. But nothing, not even the way her body reacted to seeing him naked the other time, prepared her for the tumultuous, rolling waves of pleasure pulsing through her body now. Or for the way she wanted, she craved something more.

His mouth was hot and his tongue rough against hers. Her body wept in that place between her legs and throbbed there with every caress of his tongue as some pulse within her matched his every touch.

He lifted his head in spite of her effort to hold him to her and laughed. 'Worry not. I am not through kissing you yet.'

She lost her breath at that promise and allowed him leave to move as he would. Ciara could not have imagined the pleasure of the way his beard felt as he kissed back down her body, teasing and rubbing her now-sensitive flesh. She waited and hoped he would kiss her breasts again and when he did, she arched over and over under his mouth, gasping at the feel of such a thing.

His mouth tormented her, soothed her and then tortured her over and over as anticipation built. Towards something, however—she knew not what. When his mouth moved from her breasts and then downwards, downwards towards that aching place, she stopped breathing. He laughed, the beast! He knew what he was doing to her and enjoyed it.

She reached out for his head, grabbing his hair and threading her hands through it, just as he kissed her mound. Ciara thought she might have moaned aloud then, but lost herself completely when he urged her to open to him. Her body and legs understood, spreading as he moved to kneel there.

Then he stopped.

Opening the eyes she didn't even realise she'd clenched shut, she could see him staring at her. Staring there, between her legs. She tried to bring her legs together, but his body, his hard thighs blocked her. She leaned up on her elbows and tried to cover herself with her hand, but the wicked, wicked grin on his face stopped her.

'Another place to kiss, Ciara.'

She felt the heat rush into her cheeks then. 'Surely not?' she whispered. Lips and mouths were for kissing. That place was for...

'Ah, aye, lass. 'Tis a splendid place to show you the true pleasure of a kiss.'

He kissed the inside of her thighs, tickling them with his beard's growth and then moved closer and closer to the heated flesh that throbbed already. He smiled at her as he placed his mouth...*there*.

Her mind retreated from the intensity of the pleasure from it. Her body gave in and she lost control. Lips. Tongue. Teeth. Driving her mad and pushing her body and her soul on to something more. Ciara fell back on the bed and simply felt it all.

Spiralling pleasure, rolling through her body and mixing with tendrils of need and heat and hunger for him and what he did to her. She opened wider to him, allowing him whatever he wanted. Her body arched, pressing against his mouth harder, forcing his tongue deeper into that place.

She did scream then as her body shivered and trembled against his mouth. Something deep within her, something wound so tight she could not breath, loosened in an instant and wave upon wave of ecstasy rushed through her blood and into every part of her. She lost herself in that moment and only later did she realise that he lay now at her side, whispering to her.

Ciara did not know she cried until she felt him wiping the tears from her cheeks, kissing them away. After such abandonment of control, she did not know if she could meet his gaze.

A gentle touch of his lips on hers convinced her to risk it.

And love shone back at her.

Chapter Eighteen

She was embarrassed.

She was magnificent.

He'd watched as she gave herself over to him and allowed him to give her pleasure. And he'd touched her with nothing but his mouth. He ached for release, but he would not seek it now—he would not bury himself deep within her still-pulsing flesh no matter how much he longed to do so. When her hand brushed against him, he hissed at the near-painful touch. Ciara pushed up on her elbows and looked at him, making it react.

'Did I hurt you?' she asked.

He laughed and shook his head. 'You did not.'

'But you did not...?' She reached for him

and he swore he would spill it if she uttered another word about it.

'Nay. Worry not about it, lass.'

He began to sit up, to move away, when she put her hand on his chest and pushed him down. ''Tis my turn to kiss you,' she said, bold now, embarrassment clearly forgotten.

'You will kill me.'

She laughed at that and shrugged. 'Let us find out.'

No threat uttered by foe and friend ever filled him with such terror. The thought of her mouth on him, on his flesh, made him shake. She laughed at that, too, before kneeling over and staring at his body. He closed his eyes and threw his arm across them. Mayhap if he did not watch he could control himself?

The first touch of her mouth, on his nipples, proved that this battle would require every ounce of will within him and he still might lose. But when she moved lower and he felt the heat of her mouth and the tickling trail of her hair on his thighs, he knew he could never win.

She learned quickly, imitating everything he'd done with deadly accuracy. Unsure of what to do, she touched the tip of her tongue to him and he reacted suddenly.

'Bad?' she asked in a throaty voice.

'Good,' he growled back. 'Too good.'

The witch laughed and applied her newly found skills to torturing him until he begged her for more. She traced a path with her wet, hot tongue.

Ciara would drive him insane from the pleasure. She used her lips and tongue against him as he had on her flesh and he even felt the edges of her teeth graze along the length of him. He knew his release was not far off.

That was when she realised she could take him in her mouth. She opened her lips, surrounded the head of his cock and pushed down until she took most of it inside. Her innocence was demonstrated once again when she paused and he realised she did not know what to do next. He could have died a happy man in that position, but he urged her on.

Tavis deserved the torment he received, for though new at this, it took her little time to master the movements and bring him to within moments of release. He allowed himself to enjoy the feel of her mouth tightening around him, but he lifted her head.

'I think I like kissing,' she said with a smile.

'Then think of how much you will like the rest of it.'

The words were out before he thought them through, but for a fleeting moment they both realised that it would not be him doing the rest of it with her.

'Come, Ciara. You should get home before you are missed.'

He slid from the bed and gathered up her clothes, only then realising that she did not move. Well, she did move, but that was only to stretch her body like a cat, elongating her spine and rolling on to her belly, giving him a glimpse of her beautifully sculpted arse. Her long, blonde curls swirled over her body, hiding just enough to be enticing.

'My parents believe I am spending the night at Elizabeth's,' she explained. 'A last night alone with a dear, dear friend.'

He did not like deceiving his friend and mentor, but the alternative was a slow and agonising death at his hands for even touching his daughter this way.

'You did not touch me with your hands,' she said. He'd hoped she'd not notice that. Leave it to her to pick up on it.

'You asked me for a kiss,' he said, walking

to the bed and holding out her clothes. 'You got your kiss.'

'You make it sound like a chore,' she said, laughing. 'I thought men enjoyed tupping.'

He sat next to her and tossed the clothes on a stool. 'Men do. But we are not...tupping. I told you—'

'I understand your boundaries, Tavis. And I thank you for them. But will touching me cross that line?'

'You are killing me by inches!'

'Then we can talk instead.' She held out the weapon and he suspected she knew it would work. It did.

He turned and was on her before she could react. He lay over her, enjoying the feel of her. He eased one leg between hers from the back and slid it high, grazing the hair and rubbing until it eased up against her womanly flesh.

She sighed and leaned back against him, exposing her breasts to him. He slid his hand across them, caressing them until she arched against him. Positioned as she was, her neck was open to him and he leaned down and kissed her there, enjoying the way she shivered in his grasp.

Every sound she made pushed him to pleasure her more. He moved so that she lay half on him and eased both hands around her waist so he could stroke the folds between her legs. She lifted her leg over his, giving him access and he slipped his fingers along the wet flesh. Her breathing became shallower with each touch and she shifted restlessly against him. This time she and her body knew what to expect and she responded to each caress. He found the little bud buried in the folds and touched it. She moaned and opened more to him. He kissed her neck and bit down gently on the cord of muscle there. Her indrawn breath was her reply.

'Now, Tavis, now!' she demanded.

He did as she asked and moved faster and faster against her readied flesh until she fell apart in his arms.

It was magnificent to see and to feel. Neither of them moved for several minutes and it felt incredible to hold her like this.

'Now it is time for you to go, Ciara,' he whispered as he relaxed his hold on her and rolled away.

But she followed him and slid her arms around him. 'Now? Now when you are ready?'

She could feel the moment his resistance melted, for he turned in her arms and slid up against the headboard of the bed, giving her complete access to his body.

'Here, like this,' he said, as she knelt next to him and wrapped her hands around him.

'Like churning butter,' she said, intent on her purpose once she got the movements in a smooth rhythm.

He laughed then, leaned over and kissed her on the mouth. It made her lose her pacing, but she got it back. He did not laugh after that. He may have panted, he may have moaned, but he did not laugh...

Later, Tavis took one of her hands and slid his fingers between hers.

'Now you must go,' he whispered, kissing her knuckles.

'Aye.'

'Do you have regrets about coming here now?' he asked softly, not letting go of her hand.

She started to answer, but what good would it do? So she shook her head. She began to sit up and he helped her this time.

Ciara knew she was not done here yet, even if Tavis did not. She'd come here with two purposes in mind and only one was accomplished. Accomplished well and wonderfully and now she would never have to wonder what it would be like to find pleasure in his bed. But the more serious task lay ahead.

They dressed in silence and he poured her a cup of ale before she left. Ciara knew he would follow her back to make certain she made it safely and without being recognised—he could not help himself. She turned to him before lifting the latch and stopped.

'I have one more request of you, Tavis.'

'Do not ask me to watch you marry him, Ciara. I cannot do that, even for you.'

She smiled, her eyes filling with tears. She shook her head and glanced away for a moment. 'Nay, not that.'

'Then what do you ask?' he said quietly.

'Tell me of Saraid's death at your hands. I would know why she haunts you even these years later.'

'Ciara,' he said, his voice pleading with only that word for her to stop.

'I would know why the woman you loved above all keeps your heart and soul bound to her, even in death. You owe me at least that.'

He grimaced at her, but it did not put her off.

'Do you know that I plotted to trip her on her way to the church for your wedding? To keep her from marrying so that you would wait for me?' Tears gathered once more, but she smiled through them. 'Elizabeth and I were ready to lunge and bring her down.' She nodded then. 'Now when I look back, I realise it was a grievous error on my part not to have done it.'

'You did not?' He narrowed his gaze and laughed then. 'You did? What stopped you?'

'I saw the way you looked at her from your place by the door.' She took in and released a breath. 'I knew then that that was what love looked like.'

'I did love her,' he admitted the obvious.

'You looked at me that way on our journey to Perthshire. I saw it then.'

'I cannot deny the love I feel for you. I just cannot put you in the same position I did Saraid.'

'Tell me, Tavis. Explain how you killed her.' She dropped her shawl around her shoulders and sat down in his chair. 'I am not leaving, not giving myself to another man instead of the one I love, until I understand what keeps your heart imprisoned.'

'She was carrying our bairn,' he said, rubbing his hands through his hair and turning away from her to stare into the fire that now burned low in the hearth. 'And she had terrible fears about it. Terrible. She would beg me every night not to leave her alone. Not to let her die.' He glanced at her with bleak eyes and then continued. 'God forgive me, but I tired of it. She became too scared to leave the cottage. Too frightened to do most anything. She would not travel with me. Would not ride a horse. Would not...'

Ciara did not remember this at all. Too young to realise the true intimacy between a man and his wife. 'What happened?'

'I swore to keep her safe. I swore she would not die, I would not let her die.' He shook his head again, but did not meet her gaze then. 'Connor asked me to see to a task for him that would take me from the village for a day, maybe two, and I accepted the assignment. I could have assigned someone else, knowing how frightened Saraid was—I should have. But, sweet Christ, I needed to be away from her for a short time. I could not breathe, I could not...'

He walked over and splashed more ale in a cup for himself and drank it down. She could feel the pain pouring out of him with each passing moment. He was reliving this dark time in the telling of it.

'We argued. We argued badly and I left her behind. Told her I would be back whenever I got back,' he admitted in a tortured voice. 'I did not know…I had no idea…' He ran his hand through his hair and stared at her with bleak eyes. 'I goaded her into something she should not have done.'

Ciara went to him, kneeling before him and taking his hand in hers. He needed to tell this and release the pain he carried deep, deep inside.

'I carried out my duty. It was a day's ride away. I was returning when I found her.'

'You found her? Where was she?'

'Her pains began after our argument. Instead of calling for the midwife or one of the women, she got on a horse and followed me. She caught up with me a few hours from here and I was still angry. I ordered her off, demanded she return here without hearing her out and then I rode off full of my own bluster and rage.

'By the time I returned and found her there on the ground the next day, she'd bled so much there was nothing I could do for her.'

'Tavis, it was not your fault,' she said firmly. 'You did not cause her death.'

'But I did, Ciara. If I'd been more attentive. If I'd listened. If I had stayed. If I'd ridden back with her and saw to her safety, she might be alive today.'

'That is something that only the Almighty decides, Tavis. Not us. She could have died in childbirth, too. Would that have been your fault?'

'I gave her my word! Do you not understand? I swore an oath to keep her safe and I rode away.' His hands shook as much as his voice did. 'She would have had a chance if not for me and my anger. If not for me...'

He had played a part in Saraid's death, if he'd acted as he'd just described, but Ciara thought the ending might have been the same no matter what help he offered or what he did. Tavis was too controlled by his guilt and pain to accept any truth that might include his own vindication, but mayhap he would when he thought on it.

Later.

Later, when he considered the error in his decision not to put the past behind him and ignore a future he, they, could share. Or later when he learned how to forgive himself for his failings.

She stood and put her shawl up to cover her head for the walk back to Elizabeth's cottage. Well, not really to her cottage, for Elizabeth did not know of her plans this night. No one did. She would sleep in the small barn next to Elizabeth's and then return to her parents' house in the morning—none the wiser of what she'd done or where she'd been.

'I know it is too late for us, but I beg you to speak to the midwife, Gunna. She saw Saraid frequently and has a different view of things. It might help you forgive yourself.'

He was too steeped in the pain of dragged-up memories to hear anything else. 'Twas only then that she noticed the small piece of wood on the hearth's shelf. Picking it up, she recognised the shape—a heart. Instead of a horse, he'd carved something of himself for her to keep with her always. Tears trickled down her cheeks as she shook her head and walked to the doorway.

'Farewell, Tavis,' she whispered as she closed her fingers around the precious keepsake. Ciara opened the door and pulled it closed behind her and ran off down the path.

She found the barn and sneaked inside to hide for the rest of the night. Pressing herself against one wall, she wrapped the shawl around her and waited for the tears to flow.

But they did not. Instead memories of the wondrous passion they'd shared flooded back and she knew she'd done the right thing. Now, at least she could have those memories and this treasured reminder from him while she lived the life of the contented wife of James Murray.

Chapter Nineteen

The next day dawned cloudy and grey and Tavis thought it appropriate, for it matched his mood. She'd left and he sat in the chair the rest of the night, thinking about Saraid.

Not what he wanted to be thinking about.

He wanted to relive the memories of bringing Ciara to life under his mouth and with the touch of his hands. He wanted to remember the sighs and the moans and the breathless way she said his name as she found repletion. He wanted to think about the way she learned what pleased him so quickly and how she managed to bring him to climax with little more than a touch of her mouth or her hands.

Instead, every single mistake he'd made with Saraid, every mean word and thought, repeated in his head all night long. Her fears that swallowed up the woman he'd fallen in love with. Her incessant demands that drove him mad. Her desperation that increased day by day and that he could not seem to resolve. No amount of reassurance had helped. And no matter what Ciara thought, he was the cause of it.

His selfishness in needing to get away from her.

His negligence in taking her fears seriously.

His inability to care for her and to protect her from the one thing she feared most: dying.

He'd failed as a husband and as a man and Saraid had died as a result of it. Would it happen again if he allowed himself to love another? Was it a terrible flaw in his character or had he simply failed once?

He moved through the day barely aware of the goings-on around him. He finished the tasks he needed to see to and decided it was as good a time as any to speak to Connor about leaving Lairig Dubh. Connor agreed to meet him after the midday meal and invited him to join them. There would be no elaborate evening meal this night since preparations were going on for the marriage feast on the morrow.

Connor grimaced after saying it, but Tavis

simply nodded and agreed to come back later. He filled the time with training even though the skies opened and it rained for several hours. He did not really feel it and did not feel much of anything this day. The only thing in his favour was that he did not see *her* at all this day.

He climbed the stairs to Connor's chamber and found him in the middle of an argument with his wife. He could not make out the words and was waiting for things to calm inside before making his presence known, but Rurik walked up behind him and knocked.

'That could go on for some time, lad. We do not want to wait here forever,' Rurik advised.

Since he reported to Rurik and worked with him, it made sense that Connor had asked him to be part of this discussion.

When the voices did not cease, Rurik opened the door and yelled inside, 'Should we wait out here for you two to finish or can we come inside?'

Tavis shook his head. Only Rurik could, and did, get away with such behaviour. He'd shown up in Lairig Dubh with their uncle, a hulking, half-Scots, half-Norse warrior, bigger than anyone had ever seen, and pledged to Connor's service. He was the fiercest fighter and most loyal friend Connor had and could count on in any situation. Rurik had even given up his right to the earldom of Orkney to return here when he married Margriet.

So, Tavis understood why Connor allowed him such impertinence.

'We are finished,' Jocelyn shouted back, as she walked by them and slammed the door shut behind her.

Rurik knew better than to joke at this moment, so Tavis just remained silent and waited on Connor. He was pacing back and forth and cursing under his breath, clearly still carrying on the conversation with Jocelyn even though she had left in the middle of it.

'Wives!' he yelled as he slammed a cup down and filled it with ale. Rurik walked over to him, poured another cup for himself and handed one to Tavis.

'Wives!' he said, raising the cup and then emptying it in one swallow.

Tavis drank it all down without a word about wives…anyone's wife. Connor sat at his table and motioned for them to sit. Rurik remained standing, as he always did, and Tavis sat.

'You asked about a new assignment?'

'I would like to move from Lairig Dubh and

thought I could serve your needs better on one of your other holdings.'

The words were out, easier to say than he thought they'd be. He watched as Connor exchanged several glances with Rurik and waited for the reaction.

'Does this have anything to do with Ciara and James Murray?' Connor did not lack directness.

'It matters not, Connor. They will marry on the morrow and return to Perthshire. This is about me.'

'And moving will do what for you, Tavis?' Rurik asked. 'You have been my commander for some time now and I think it's the best place for you.'

'Young Dougal would be good. He is a good fighter and ready for more responsibility.'

'Why do you want this?' Connor asked again.

'I need to be away from here. I need to find a place where I am not haunted by my past every day from when I open my eyes until I close them.'

Sweet Christ! He never meant to say any of that. Not to anyone, but especially not to Connor.

'Once the wedding is done and the Murrays leave, we will speak again on this matter, Tavis. I cannot make a decision until I speak to the stewards and commanders at the other holdings.'

He stood. He did not truly expect Connor to simply approve his request, but he did not expect to be put off for so long.

'Soon, Connor,' he said. 'Make it soon,' he challenged as he nodded to Connor and Rurik as he walked towards the doorway.

'Tavis,' Connor called to him just before he opened it, 'is there anything else you need to discuss with me?'

Tavis looked from one to the other and tried to work out what they thought he needed to talk about with Connor.

'Nay, Connor. That was all.'

Connor nodded, dismissing him, and he made his way back down the stairs, only to find Jocelyn waiting for him. Still full of fire and fight from whatever she was speaking, or shouting, with Connor about, she started to ask him several questions at once and then stopped. He'd never seen her so angry. She gave up trying and climbed the stairs to their chambers.

Everyone seemed to be on edge here. Were

the plans for the wedding at fault? Or the new agreement with the Murrays? Or was something else at play that he was not privy to? No matter, he still had duties to see to until Connor made his decision.

Leaving the keep, he decided to try to get some rest tonight since he'd got none last night. Walking back to his cottage, one of the boys from the village stopped him with a message. Gunna the midwife wanted to speak to him. Since she had to leave to tend to a woman on one of the farms, could he come as soon as possible?

Had Ciara done this? She said she'd spoken to the woman. If the thought of losing her had not relieved him of his guilt in Saraid's death, why would the words of a stranger persuade him?

Tavis thanked the boy for carrying the message and almost ignored it. Did he really want to dredge up more of the pain? What did she think to accomplish by this?

I know it is too late for us, but I beg you to speak to the midwife, Gunna. She saw Saraid frequently and has a different view of things.

He did not know that Saraid had sought out the old woman. She was only months into carrying and long before she would need a midwife. She had been healthy and had no problems. Why would she seek out Gunna?

Standing there, debating this in his own thoughts, would get him nowhere. If nothing else, speaking with the old woman would simply confirm that he was right about Saraid's health.

Tavis walked through the village, past Elizabeth's cottage and down the lane to almost the edge where the old woman lived with her daughter. Knocking on the door and identifying himself, he was welcomed in. Gunna's daughter was feeding a babe and Gunna was packing supplies for the birth she was going off to attend to.

'Tavis, 'tis good to see you,' her daughter, Fia, said. Fia's husband was one of Tavis's warriors, a good man.

'Fia, you look well. The bairn?' All he could see was a small head with thick black hair pressed up against her chest.

She rubbed the bairn's head and nodded. 'Young Alpin is well,' she said. He smiled at the name chosen.

'Do you need a ride, Gunna?' Tavis asked. 'I could get a wagon,' he offered. The nearest of the farms was some distance and it would take her a goodly amount of time to walk there.

'Nay,' she said, shaking her head. 'Nessa's husband is sending his wagon shortly. Walk with me, Tavis. I meet him at the river's edge.'

Bidding Fia farewell, he walked outside with Gunna, taking the sack from her and carrying it. They walked a few paces before he asked her, 'Why did you summon me? Is there something you need?'

'Oh, you're a good lad,' she said, patting him on the back. 'Nay, I need nothing. But speaking to Ciara the other day reminded me that we never spoke after your sweet wife passed.'

'I did not know she sought your care, Gunna. She was only about five months carrying.'

'Oh, aye,' she said, pointing in the direction they needed to walk, her body waddling from side to side as they did. 'She had some fears about carrying. After all, her mam lost four bairns before delivering the three girls. And two of them died giving birth.'

Saraid had never explained her fears. He'd not known about losing sisters in childbirth.

'She never told me,' he said.

'She didna want you to ken, but she wanted me to.' She paused for a moment, staring at him. 'Did she fall from the horse? Is that how she passed?' Gunna asked.

'I found her on my way from Dalmally on the laird's business. She was bleeding heavily and said her pains had begun the day before.' He did not speak of the rest of it or expose his role in the debacle.

'I told her she might lose it. Told her not to strain or carry.'

'I did not know,' he whispered.

'You're a good lad,' Gunna said. 'But some women are not built to birth bairns. Your Saraid was one of them. She knew it, but wanted to try for you.'

'Was there anything I could have done?'

'Oh, nay,' she said, shaking her head. ''Twas in God's hands to decide. Even if I was next to her when the pains started, I couldna saved her. The bairn would not have lived that early born.'

It was just as Ciara had told him. Nothing would have mattered. Nothing could have saved Saraid.

That did not lessen his guilt in her death and in the manner of her death, for she'd died alone, in terror and pain, while he rode off in anger. He'd spent years regretting what he'd done. Spent years with guilt weighing down his soul for killing her. His heart locked away in fear and pain.

Tavis would rather have been at her side, soothing the fears and holding her than to know she lay by the road for hours by herself. She was incoherent by the time they arrived back here. The healer had visited and given her a potion for the pain, but nothing could stop the bleeding that eventually took her life.

If anything happens to me, you must go on.

Saraid's words from his dream, from early in their marriage, came back to him then. She knew. Somehow she knew. And she'd warned him, but when the time came, he did not recognise it.

Stunned, he stopped walking. He stopped thinking. When he realised he was not moving, he glanced around and found that Gunna was gone. Shaking his head, he looked in the distance and saw her on a wagon many yards away—he never even realised she'd left.

He needed to think about all this and he did not know where to go. The one person he most wanted to speak to was the one he could not. She had known. And she pointed him in the right direction to find out and accept it for himself, freeing himself from the past.

I know it is too late for us...

Even knowing it would not benefit her, she'd protected him in a way he'd never been able to do for her. She'd been a better friend to him, in spite of his efforts to hold her away, than he'd been to her, even in the early years.

And she loved him enough to free him from his past and to let him go. To make him understand that his failure to one woman did not mean he would fail everyone, even while he failed her.

Tavis went back to his cottage where the echoes and ghosts of the past still haunted and tried to figure out how to right a life that had gone so wrong. But he feared that he was indeed too late to correct all his mistakes and to learn from his past ones. Only when he noticed that his latest carving—the one he'd promised to make for her—was gone, did he dare allow himself to have any hope at all.

Ciara had had no idea that pleasure could ache so much.

Or mayhap it was from sleeping up against a wall, wrapped in only a plaid shawl? As she'd uncurled herself, her body had let her know that, whatever caused the aches, she would suffer for it.

Waking to find only darkness outside, she'd wondered if she'd awoken before dawn, but after stumbling to the door on legs that were numb from being under her all night, she'd discovered the sun had risen after all. Thick clouds covered the sky and rumbles of thunder rolled within them.

Her stomach had added a few more, reminding her that she had not eaten since yesterday. And she'd had some quite strenuous exercise since then.

That had made her smile, regardless of the aches and pains.

There were places on her body that she had never known could feel the way he made them feel. The rapture that women had talked about, whispering amongst themselves, was no longer a mystery to her. Tavis had awakened her body and those senses and overwhelmed them. As she walked, the place between her legs actually throbbed as memories of his intimate caresses there returned. Her breasts tingled and in her mind she could still see his mouth on her.

She'd made her way home and, after hiding the wooden heart inside her trunk, Ciara had broken her fast with her family, explaining that she wanted to be home on this last day before leaving them. Her mother's eyes had filled with tears while her sister asked if she could have Ciara's bedchamber now that she would be the oldest. Ciara had allowed these joyful moments to wash over her for soon, very soon, they would be over and she would be gone.

Her mother had made her favourite porridge, extra creamy this morn, and even her father had joined them and lingered there longer than usual. She wondered if they could tell that she was somehow different this morning. She felt different from inside out. A woman now where a girl stood before. Though that last step to womanhood would be on the morrow.

Finally, everyone had set about on their day's tasks and she began to pack for both the next night, which would be spent in a chamber in the keep, and for the journey—nay, move to James's home. She stumbled now just as she had a few weeks ago over what to take and what to leave behind, but now it meant letting go of whatever remained here in the chamber. She was touching the carvings when her mother came in. She did not know she was crying until her mother touched her shoulder and took her in her arms.

'There now, sweetling,' she soothed. 'Soon you will have your own bairns and I can send these along for them.'

'I do not know why I am so weepy, Mother. 'Tis not as though I did not know this day would come.'

'Knowing it approached and having it here are two different matters.'

Ciara leaned back and searched her mother's face. 'I do not know how you did it. Taking on everything you did. Seeing to me. Then marrying Papa and coming to a new village, a new clan and a whole new life.'

'I married a good man, just as you will.'

Her mother stroked her back, touching her hair and combing it with her fingers in a calming motion she would miss. She was thinking of the man she was not marrying, so she remained silent in her mother's embrace.

'You are at peace with this marriage?' her mother finally asked. Leaning back, she nodded.

'I am.' Her mother kissed her on both cheeks and released her. 'There is much good that will be gained by seeing it through.'

'Then you must get dressed, for there is much to do. Jocelyn is waiting for our help.' Her mother did not dally, leaving and pulling the door closed as she went.

Looking at the wooden animals that stared back at her, she wondered if Tavis would speak to Gunna or remain mired in his grief and guilt. She touched each of them, offering up a short prayer for his happiness, and wondered if he'd even noticed the heart was missing from his shelf.

The day moved quickly by her. She spent time with James at the keep. Even he joined in the efforts to prepare for the wedding feast. His parents clearly did not think it appropriate for anyone but the servants to do such work and they left rather than watch their son doing menial labour or before they could be coerced into helping in some way.

Ciara had learned long ago that she could not sit for endless hours sewing or embroidering or reading aloud from prayer books or other such womanly arts. Oh, she had the abilities and skills to do such work, but not the patience for it. She would rather be riding or walking or debating with her father or playing chess against her mother. As she watched the Murrays leaving, she wondered if she would change once she was under their roof or if they would make allowances for her Highland upbringing.

The families ate a mid-day meal together, light fare since the cooks were preparing the roasts and stews and fish and sweets that would feed them all after the wedding and they had not the time nor the hands needed to cook a full meal for mid-day as well. She sat next to James, who grew quiet as a few bawdy toasts were made. There would be more, many more and much bawdier, during the feast, but that was expected.

She looked up at the corner tower where their bedchamber was. Her mother and James's mother had prepared it for their use and the bed was now covered in clean linens. Her mother's wink told her other pleasant surprises awaited them there.

Soon, their tasks complete, she walked with her mother and Elizabeth back to the village.

'Will you stay with me this night, Elizabeth?' she asked as they reached the split in the path. 'I would love your company on my last night before my marriage.'

'As long as you do not stay up all night chattering away and get no sleep,' her mother warned.

'I...I cannot,' Elizabeth murmured, looking away. 'I am needed at home.' Her voice shook, filled with some unnamed emotion. 'Forgive me, Ciara,' she whispered.

Ciara hugged her and shook her head. 'There is nothing to forgive. We will have much time together when we live in Perthshire, Elizabeth. No worrying over this one night.'

Elizabeth stepped back and nodded. She left without another word to either of them.

'Weddings and funerals bring out the best and worst in people, Ciara. Emotions run high for so many reasons.'

All throughout the day she had hoped. She had hoped he'd spoken to Gunna. She had hoped he would overcome his fears. She had hoped that he would... None of it mattered, for the night finally arrived and he did not.

Her trunks were packed, her clothing folded neatly within them, ready for the trip to begin her married life with James. Though she wanted to give in to some need within her soft heart and bring the newly carved heart along with her, she feared she was holding on to the past too firmly and let it remain in its place there.

In spite of knowing that it would offer some measure of comfort for the days ahead, she told herself repeatedly in that moment that she must leave it behind. Tavis had been her first friend and she would never forget him, but 'twas time to relegate him to her past. Anger surged past the pain in her veins and made her want to pound her fists and stamp her feet over the fact that he could, and had, let her go...again.

No matter that, she took a breath and walked away from the shelf that held so many memories. She had to put aside her hopes for something more between them now, for to do otherwise would guarantee not contentedness, but bitterness in her marriage. She wondered through the day and into the evening if a day would pass in which she did not think of him. Each time such a thought arose, she convinced herself that a time would indeed come.

Her mother and sister joined her in her bed for a while, probably sensing her nervousness, and they talked into the night. She missed Elizabeth's presence, but Ciara sensed that something was wrong and would speak to her in the morning to settle it. Thinking back on the last several days, she tried to remember if she'd said or done anything that was hurtful to her friend and could think of nothing. Well, mayhap her mother had the right of it—weddings brought out all kinds of emotions.

When her mother handed her a cup of steaming tea, she knew there was something in it to help her sleep. She sipped it slowly and allowed her mother to tuck her under the covers for the last time.

Whether the potion's effect or her heart's, her sleep was filled with the most wondrous dreams of the life ahead of her. The wedding, the feast, the first night together and even dreams of her first child. Tears and joy in every scene as they spun out through the whole night.

When Ciara woke in the morning and recognised the day, she realised that every single one of her dreams had the wrong husband in them. She'd dreamt the night away married to Tavis, while James would be the one awaiting her as she walked down the church's aisle.

Chapter Twenty

The wedding would take place just before noon with the feast following for…well, for as long as it took. Her mother moved quietly through the cottage this morn as though not to disturb her thoughts. And strangely she had few.

These last days had wiped her clean of regrets and had given her the resolve to do the duty she owed to her parents and to the MacLerics. Now, knowing everything her mother had given up and suffered for her over these years, she thought that marrying James was a small thing to do in return.

Elizabeth had not arrived yet and Ciara wondered over her lateness. They'd planned to prepare themselves here and walk to the chapel together with her parents, meeting James and his parents at the entrance. Then together she and James would enter the church and leave as man and wife.

They'd not yet made their final plans, but his parents mentioned travelling to Glasgow before returning to their home. How strange would it be to travel now with a husband? One to sleep with at night. One to care for during the day. She turned to watch her parents as they spoke quietly and wondered how long it took them to fall in love after their precipitous wedding. After hearing more of the story from them and comparing it to what she knew as childish memories, she understood now that more had happened between them than what she knew. And she doubted now their marriage began on less than a rocky start.

When Elizabeth still did not arrive, her mother helped her dress and, along with her younger sister, they decorated her hair with flowers. The tears in her father's eyes when he watched from the doorway of her chamber told her this was the right thing to do.

For everyone involved.

Soon, the time came to leave for the chapel. Walking between her parents, they made their way to Elizabeth's cottage first to find her.

Ciara did not remember a change of plans, but in the emotional upheaval over this last week or so, she could have missed it. The expression of shock on Elizabeth's mother's face told her it was not her failure at all.

'Is Elizabeth ready, Edana?' her mother asked.

Edana shook her head, glancing from one to the other and back again to her. 'I thought she was with you already, Ciara. Her dress is gone. She left last night, saying she would spend the night with you, to calm your fears over your coming marriage as a friend should.'

'But she told me you had need of her here last night when I asked her to stay,' Ciara said.

'Come, Ciara,' her father said, squeezing her hand to reassure her. 'Once we get to the chapel, I will send men out to look for her. She may even be there waiting for you now and we will have no cause for worry. Mayhap in the excitement of the day, your plans were confused.'

Ciara nodded. His advice seemed sound. Elizabeth would indeed be at the church waiting. Once they were standing next to each other, it would all be good and Elizabeth would stand witness to her vows to James and travel with her to their home.

As they got closer to the gates, others gathered to watch them walk by, calling out greetings and good wishes and then following them along. By the time they entered the yard and made their way to the small church, a large crowd was behind her. Though not her family by birth, they had accepted her and treated her as one of them. They were not loud and unruly, but a sense of joy ran through the crowd as little girls handed her flowers and touched her dress and hair.

Ciara allowed herself only one final moment of weakness as she walked, peering off down the path that would lead to Tavis's cottage. If either of her parents noticed, neither indicated it. They made their way to the chapel without pause then.

And they arrived at the church doors just as the rains came.

''Tis good luck for the bride when it rains on her wedding day,' someone called out. Laughter followed since everyone knew someone would have said the same thing if the sun shone.

'Go inside,' her mother directed. 'We can wait out the shower there.'

Ciara followed and let most of the crowd pass to get inside. Waiting at the doorway, she looked for Elizabeth again, but did not see her there or in the yard.

'Father, she is not here,' she said, as her father searched the faces in the crowd for her friend.

'I will ask Father Micheil if she has been here and send someone to the hall to seek her out.'

A concerned glance shared between her parents made her worried. Elizabeth would not miss her wedding. She would not. Not if she could help it.

Had she taken ill somewhere? Was she safe?

Her mother took her hand and squeezed it. 'He will find her. All will be well,' she said. 'After all, it is my beloved daughter's wedding day. Rain or no, Elizabeth or no, this is a special day and one not to be marred for you.' Smoothing her hair from her face, her mother cupped her cheek in her palm and smiled. 'No worries allowed this day for you, sweetling.'

The rains worsened as Ciara stood waiting for James. He would be dressed in his finest garments and would look handsome as he walked with her down the aisle. They would say the words binding their lives. He would care for her as her father had her mother. They would work together in their endeavours. All would be well.

So why did she have the terrible urge to do something embarrassing right now? Why did she want to scream and run from this church and from all the arrangements and agreements? To do the one thing that James had asked her not to do this day?

'A momentary panic,' her mother said, as though reading her thoughts. 'Take a deep breath and it will pass.'

'Did it happen to you, Mother?' she asked, doing as her mother suggested.

'Aye,' she said, smiling. 'Your father had no idea of what he'd walked into with my family. He was forced to marry me, not knowing the half of it.'

'Forced? I cannot imagine him forced to anything.'

'Ah, he was tied by the words and contracts he so enjoys writing. No choice but to marry me and take us both away.'

'And look how it turned out for you two,' she said, knowing that there were not two people who loved each other more than her parents did.

'Aye, Ciara,' she said. 'Look how we turned out.'

It was her mother's way of soothing her without making it obvious. Things would work out for her and James. Things could be good between them. She focused on those thoughts over the next minutes as they waited.

Those minutes flowed by with no sign of Elizabeth, her father, the Murrays or an end to the rain, either. Now she was getting worried. The people waiting inside the church grew restless as well as they noticed that something was not right. Questions and whispers echoed through the stone building and she heard some of them. Then, when she looked out the door once more, she discovered the one man she never thought to see here.

The one man who told her he could not attend, even for her.

Tavis.

He stood in the rain, halfway between the church and the gates, arguing with her father.

In the rain.

She shook her head and would have gone to see what they fought over, when her mother grabbed her and pulled her back.

'You are to marry James, Ciara. Let your father see to whatever business Tavis has.'

But she could not tear her eyes from the scene. Her mother, sensing trouble, took her by her hand and led her further inside the church, away from the doors and from the spot where she could watch Tavis. 'Here, now, Father Micheil has brought a chair for your use while we wait out the storm.'

Ciara had no choice unless she pushed out of her mother's grasp and ran out of the church. And what good would that do her or James? He did not want to be embarrassed here today. Had he known this would happen? She shook her head, clearing her thoughts and reminding herself that she had chosen this path, She had given her word. So, she told herself now as her stomach tightened with worry, she would just be patient.

Except that she was not a patient person.

'What is keeping James? His parents should be here by now.'

'I do not know, sweetling,' her mother said. Mayhap sensing that Ciara was nigh to doing something less patient than sitting here among the MacLeries waiting for her groom to arrive, her mother made an offer. 'I will go to your father and see what is happening.'

After calling her other daughter, Beitris, over to sit with Ciara, her mother walked away, speaking in low tones to this one and that one who all asked the same questions of her. Murmuring some replies she could not hear, Ciara watched as it took some minutes for her mother to make it to the door of the church. No sooner had she left than the crowd all began chattering and looking at the doorway.

Believing that James and his parents had arrived, she stood and waited for her parents to come back. Tavis stood in the back, outlined in the doorway, half in and half out, still arguing with her father. Everyone there wanted to hear the conversation and quieted so they did not miss any details or interesting bits.

'Tavis, do not do this,' Duncan warned. 'There is too much at stake. For Ciara and for the clan.'

'I will leave it in her hands, Duncan,' he said, loudly enough for everyone to hear.

Her hands? What was he doing?

Tavis pushed his way through the crowd towards her with her parents close behind him. Though everyone began to shift to let him through, they stayed close. Good gossip was good for years and none in the MacLerie clan would ever miss a chance to witness whatever this was.

'The papers are signed, she is as good as married to him,' Duncan argued as they strode towards her. He caught Tavis by the arm and pulled him away. Or tried to. 'You will break her heart doing this, Tavis,' he said.

'Doing what, Father?' she asked, standing now to meet him, them. Her mother tried to whisper to her father, but he shook her off and stood between her and Tavis.

'The laird stands behind this marriage. Will you break from the clan over her?'

He...he...wanted what?

'If she will have me.'

Confused, she looked at him and saw the love in his gaze once more. But now, there was no guilt and no pain sharing the place in his heart and she was glad of it.

'Tavis, what is this about?' she asked, as silence reigned inside the stone church.

Clasping her hands tightly, trying to prepare for whatever admission he would make before he walked from her life forever, she crushed the flowers she forgot were in her grasp.

'You were right, lass,' he said. 'About so many things.'

'A woman does like to hear that, lad!' someone called out from the crowd. Everyone laughed, but his green eyes darkened and his expression never changed from deadly serious.

'You are the right woman for me,' he said, pausing as though trying to remember what he wanted to say. Instead, his next words shocked her as he said them.

'You are an educated woman, one who can read and write in five languages and one who can understand contracts and negotiating. You are accomplished in skills and knowledge that most men knew not of. You are intelligent, quick-witted and any man would be glad to have you as wife.'

They were the words she'd spoken to him when asking him to marry her that night. The night that ended in pain and humiliation for her. But he continued now and added something not said between them yet.

'And you love me, Ciara. I know you do, lass. As I love you,' he said, smiling then.

'Tavis, there is more to this than love,' her father warned.

'Treaties,' he growled out. 'And I will be

outlawed for interfering with the laird's business.' He turned and faced her parents. 'But you faced that decision, too, Duncan. You could have walked away from Marian all those years ago. Did the threat of losing all of this…' he motioned his hand to indicate everything MacLerie '…did that threat keep you from claiming her?'

Her parents looked at each other for only a moment, but she knew they understood his argument.

'You made me see the truth of my failures of my past, Ciara. But your faith in me showed that I can be a better man in the future. Ciara, I want you to be my future. You already have my heart—will you have the rest of me?'

She smiled at his mention of his heart, telling her he knew she'd taken the wooden one as well as the true one within him. Ciara began to speak, but her father stopped her.

'Ciara, think about this. If you accept him, you will lose everything you have known. If the laird chooses, he can exile you both or even execute Tavis for his actions. The Murrays could go to war over this. Is it worth the cost you will pay? Is it?' he asked solemnly.

All it took was one glance at her parents to

understand. 'Was it?' she asked her mother. 'Was it worth it?'

Her mother's eyes filled with tears, but she smiled through them and nodded her head. The question meant something different to her than most listening thought it did, but her mother comprehended her true meaning. 'It was, sweetling,' she whispered as she took her father's hand in hers. 'It is.'

Love *was* worth whatever the cost. Whether love for a defenceless child or for a dearest friend, or for the man you had loved all your life, love was worth the cost. 'Twas that love that had allowed her to hope for a future with him, in spite of duties and honour and responsibilities. Could she now refuse all of that?

'I will have you, Tavis,' she said quietly.

The mayhem that those words caused tore through the small building and she thought the wooden rafters above their heads shook at the noise. Then the MacLeries gathered there inside the church erupted into cheering and Tavis finally took her in his arms and kissed her. Not a nice kiss—she felt him possess her and felt the promise of the claim he would make on her body later in that caress of his mouth on hers.

But when things settled down, it was her

father who brought their attention back to the realities of the day.

'The laird will have to make a decision, Ciara,' he warned. 'It will not be as simple as declaring yourself free of your betrothal.' He would know since he'd written the contracts himself.

'Then find a way, Peacemaker,' Tavis said. 'Come, let us go to Connor and get his decision,' he said, wrapping his hand around hers and not letting go of it. 'I cannot allow another man to claim my woman as his wife. Not while I yet live,' he swore, kissing her hand and turning towards the door.

'The laird!' someone yelled from the back of the church. 'Connor is here!' Another and another called out his name, but Rurik was the one Ciara could see.

Apparently they would face their fate sooner rather than later. The crowd parted, allowing Connor and Jocelyn and Rurik through. Looking behind them, Ciara noticed that the Murrays followed as well. But James was not with them.

What had happened?

The laird walked first to Father Micheil and spoke to him privately. All she could see was shaking heads and nodding between the two men. Glancing at the laird's wife and at Lord and Lady Murray, she only noticed that none of them would meet her eyes. She could not imagine how horrified they must be to be treated so before the MacLeries and by this turn of events. Finally, Connor called her parents and the Murrays together and spoke to them.

Would her father speak for her and Tavis? Would he defend their choice and barter for their future with his laird? Her hands shook, but Tavis put his arm around her, holding her close. Choosing him was the right thing and she would stand by her choice, even if it meant leaving Lairig Dubh. Finally, *finally*, the laird motioned for everyone to attend his words.

They would discover their fate now.

'I love you, lass,' Tavis whispered to her. 'I can never thank you enough for making me see the truth and realise I could not live without you before it was too late.'

'What will he do, Tavis?'

Tavis knew the laird better than she did. Would he allow this insult to his rights as laird or would he punish them both for daring it? Connor stood tall and looked over the crowd with his gaze falling on her first. As he shook his head, regret entered his gaze and it worried her.

'What a sad state of affairs this is,' he began. 'We negotiated in good faith to make the Murrays our allies and to join them to our clan and now we learn of this despicable act.'

Ciara could not help it—she trembled at his words. She'd never heard him speak so seriously and it terrified her. Their decision, based on their own feelings and needs, now threatened to cause a war.

'My lord—' Lord Murray interrupted, stepping forwards, but Connor waved him off.

'The betrothal was negotiated and a dowry paid to you so that your son would marry one of our own, Murray. That cannot be disputed.'

This was not good. Ciara leaned against Tavis and held her breath. Where was James? He should be here in the middle of these discussions, but she did not see him at all.

'Nay, my lord, I do not dispute that. But, I had no idea, my lord. We will make whatever concessions you ask if you will but allow this to be settled peacefully.'

Ciara stared at Lord Murray and realised that he was more frightened than she was. Why did he fear the laird's anger? Puzzled, she pulled away a bit from Tavis and looked at James's parents.

'Lord Murray?' she asked. 'What has happened? Lady Murray, where is James?'

'We did not know, Ciara. We had no way to know what he would do, child,' she said, her voice filled with regret.

'What Tavis would do?' she asked, thoroughly confused.

'Nay, Ciara. Young James Murray has disgraced himself and his family this day,' Connor explained.

'James would not do something like that,' she said. 'He is honourable and stood by the betrothal. He told me so. He asked for my consent. 'Tis I who have—' Connor held up his hand and interrupted her.

'Ciara, 'tis my regrettable duty to inform you that your betrothed, their son,' he said, nodding at James's trembling parents, 'that young James Murray kidnapped your friend Elizabeth last night with every intention of forcing her into an unsanctioned marriage with him. He left a note explaining his plans and breaking the contract with you.'

Lady Murray fainted as the words that damned her only son as a dishonourable rogue echoed through the church. As she fell, Lord Murray barely caught her and laid her on the stone floor.

'My lord, I beg you to hear me out on this matter,' he called out to Connor, passing his wife's limp body on to her servants to see to.

No thoughts or words would come to her mind, so she watched silently. Tavis squeezed her hand and smiled, but she did not dare think that this would be so easy.

'We do not want war over this, my lord,' Lord Murray called out again.

Connor called for silence again.

'Let us speak privately and come to some agreement. I beg you,' Lord Murray said, bowing low.

''Twould seem young James had the courage I lacked sooner than I did,' Tavis whispered to her. 'And Elizabeth? Was she willing, do you think?'

'I think they planned this together,' she replied as she thought over all the small clues she'd missed until now. James loved someone else, just as she did, and faced the same future married to another. His questions about her consent and all the rest were his way of coming to a decision.

By now, all the MacLeries watching understood how this would play out even if the Murrays did not and, as her father's daughter, she could read it better than most could. Connor would be insulted and play that card while Murray offered a better treaty than what had been in place. To ease the insult of his son's behaviour and to soothe the mighty temper of the Beast of the Highlands, Murray would agree to concessions that he'd balked at just days ago. Connor would be magnanimous and allow the treaty to proceed, in spite of this insult.

But that did not tell her if Connor would allow them to marry or the cost of their actions.

'Come, Lord Murray,' Connor said. 'We have much to discuss.' Connor led the way out of the church towards the keep. His closest counsellors followed close behind, barely able to contain or to mask their joy at this turn of the tables.

Lady Murray was helped up by several men, who escorted her along. Lord Murray stopped before Ciara as they passed her and shook his head.

'I am so sorry, my dear. I cannot explain what got into James that he would do such a thing. Such a disgrace. And to leave you like this at the altar. Terrible. Terrible,' he said, hurrying off to follow Connor.

'I must go with them,' her father said.

'I will come,' Tavis said, turning to her. 'I will speak to Connor.'

'Nay, Tavis,' her father said. 'Remain here with Ciara and I will find out what he plans to do. I wonder if he knew what would happen before he arrived here?'

Not waiting for an answer, he left, calling out to Rurik and a few of the men to clear the church. Within a short time, the church was empty save for her, Tavis and Father Micheil, who remained kneeling before the altar, praying.

Ciara sank on to the chair, as the enormity of everything that had happened rolled over her. Now, with a few minutes of privacy, she turned to Tavis.

'Did Connor know?' she asked quietly.

'He might have had an inkling of my plans,' Tavis admitted, with a smirk. 'I went to him early this morn and told him I needed his support.'

'You did? He could have…he could have…' The possible scenarios all spun out in her mind—very few of them ended well for a man who disobeyed his laird and caused dishonour to his clan.

'I would never let my laird enter a battle un-armed or without the correct weapons at hand, Ciara. I did not know how it would play out, but I expected Connor to have my back as I have had his all these years in his service. I pledged my loyalty and obedience to him, no matter his decision about what happens to us.'

Ciara liked the way *us* sounded to her when he said it.

'You are certain about this?' she asked.

'I spoke to Gunna as you said to,' he whispered. 'She told me the truth about Saraid's condition. I had no idea.'

'It was not your fault,' she reminded him.

'I was so mired in guilt, it never occurred to me to ask Gunna or ask anyone about her.' He kissed her hand and shook his head. 'I did not dare believe that I could be a better man until you made me face the fear I carried.'

She smiled then in spite of the tears that burned in her eyes and threatened to turn her into the ugly mess she became when crying. Still, there had been other things standing in their way.

'But what about the rest of your objections? You objected to my education, my wealth, my abilities and other things as well as not being able to love me.'

He laughed then and she loved the sound of it. For a long time she did not think he would ever smile at her as he did now.

'I was intimidated by all the things you can do that I cannot,' he admitted.

'James said the same thing to me.'

'Did he? When?'

'A few days ago. I think he was considering this when we talked. Elizabeth interrupted us.'

'I guess I am glad you frightened him off, then.'

'I am, too. I would have done it sooner if I'd known.'

He kissed her then. Not the way he wanted to, for they were in a house of God, but there would be time for that later. Once all this was settled and he knew if they stayed or went, he would speak to Father Micheil about marrying them first. He wanted her as his before another day passed if it was possible.

'I could work with you on learning your letters and numbers, you know,' she offered.

'There are others skills of yours that I wish

to concentrate on, Ciara,' he said honestly. Not the best thing to say in a house of God, but it was in his thoughts.

'Tavis!' she whispered, putting her hand over his mouth. 'Father might hear you!'

'I was thinking of your skills in playing chess,' he said with a wink. 'What wicked deeds were you thinking about?'

Now, all those thoughts entered his mind and he could not wait to claim her completely, body and soul, as his. Though after her enthusiasm a night ago, he considered that he might not survive the experience. He wouldna mind dying in trying, though.

They sat then in the silence with Father Micheil's whispered prayers echoing around them and Tavis offered up a few of his own. He did not want to rip her from everyone she loved for that was one advantage of his proposal over James's—she could stay with those who loved her and whom she loved. But, he did not want to be the cause of strife between Duncan and Connor, either.

Still, he thanked the Almighty for allowing him to see the blindness that he'd been living in and that she had made sure he discovered the truth. He could not have helped Saraid, no matter what or when it happened. He was only a man. A fallible one at that. But now he had another chance to be a better man and a better husband to Ciara.

Footsteps behind them alerted them to a decision. He kissed her hand and stood to meet their fate with her at his side. But here or somewhere else, he would be with her…always.

Chapter Twenty-One

Duncan and her mother walked slowly down the aisle towards them and Tavis held his breath. Their expressions gave nothing away as they made their way to the front of the church. The old priest stopped praying and rose from his knees to join them.

'Well, Duncan. Has this been sorted out with the laird and the Murrays?' Father Micheil asked.

'Aye, Father,' Duncan said. 'Lord Murray is devastated by what James did today, but that worked to your benefit.' He looked at Tavis first, then Ciara. 'If you had come forwards sooner, I could not say that Connor would have allowed this to go forwards.'

'What did he say?' Tavis asked.

'Since Lord Murray did not know of your declaration here, Connor was able to make it look as though he was being benevolent and understanding of the weaknesses of youth. He allowed the betrothal agreement to be broken in exchange for the same provisions to stand as they'd agreed—access to the ports of Perth and Dundee through Lord Murray's contacts.'

'But why?'

'James did marry a MacLerie without his permission as laird, so Connor will provide a dowry for Elizabeth once they are found and their marriage is confirmed.'

'Is he angry?'

'Aye, he is,' Connor said from the back of the church. Jocelyn followed along, as did Rurik and his wife. Even Gair the steward and Connor's half-sister were there. 'Angry that you did not see what everyone else has seen for years, Tavis.'

'Connor, I…' Tavis tried to explain, but then he noticed that Connor did not look angry at all. 'I allowed pride and fear to stand in my way.'

'Aye, you did just that. But when you came to speak to me about your life, I knew what you must be considering. So when young James approached me about his dilemma, I may have suggested an expedient way to handle it all at once.'

Tavis shook his head. 'You did not?'

Ciara laughed at his side. 'James spoke to you? When?'

'The other day and about an hour before you came to see me, Tavis.' Connor smiled then. 'Actually, he spoke to Jocelyn.'

'The fight,' he said, remembering the argument he overheard.

'Aye,' Jocelyn said. 'The boy knew you were not happy, but planned to do your duty, Ciara, and he admitted that he had fallen in love with Elizabeth on your journey here. He could not go to his parents, so he came to me. Someone had told him that I had tamed a certain beast.'

'Why did you not say something, Connor?' Tavis asked.

'You needed to make that decision yourself, lad. If I had smoothed the way for you, and you knew it, would you know that you were willing to risk all for her?'

'His parents know none of this?' Ciara asked.

'Nay,' Connor said. 'And for his sake, I would not tell them. He will deal with them when he, they, return to Perthshire.'

'Where did they go?' Ciara asked, concerned for her friend.

'I did not ask and did not want to know.'

Wise, Tavis thought. Aware, but not directing it all. He could still deny involvement if asked, since he'd offered counsel only.

'But she went willingly? He did not force her?'

She knew the truth when the words were said. It was a love match and there was no force used. Some convincing to take the risk, but James had followed his heart.

'And now?' Ciara asked, needing to know what their fate would be.

'Lord Murray agreed that a quick and quiet wedding between you and Tavis would remove the sting of James's abandonment,' Connor said. 'He even suggested it himself. He did not wish to see you humiliated before your family.' Connor paused and met her gaze, all amusement gone from his eyes. 'If you will have him as husband?'

She tried to keep the tears from flowing, but she could not. Every dream she had ever had about Tavis could come true. The childish ones when she made her bold claim and the more serious ones made over the years since. 'Truly?'

'Here now, lass,' Tavis said, wiping her cheeks gently. 'You know how badly you cry. I would have you happy.'

'I am happy,' Ciara said.

'Father Micheil is ready now,' her father said.

'Now?' She looked at the priest, who already had his prayer book out.

'All the legalities have been seen to,' Father Micheil said.

Ciara looked around and found all of the important people in her life smiling at her and Tavis. Something more was going on here, but she did not want to question it, for fear it would disappear. So, she joined hands with Tavis and they pledged their lives together even as their hearts had been joined for years now.

They left the church and returned to the hall in the keep where the other wedding feast had been planned. If anyone thought it strange that a different groom sat at the high table than the one they'd thought would be there, no one mentioned it among all the celebrating.

Ciara danced and ate and drank with a light heart, overwhelmed by the events of the last few hours even while looking forward to the night ahead. Having been pleasured by Tavis, she could not wait for the rest of it—for him to completely lay claim to her body as her lawful husband. She would not have to be content in this marriage bed, she could be complete. The bawdy jokes now made sense to her as those around shouted out toasts and good wishes.

If she had married James, there would have been a bedding ceremony, but now with nothing to prove to outsiders and with no grants of land and cattle attached to their marriage, she and Tavis could retire privately to the room above. Not certain when that would be, she enjoyed the festivities.

Later, while many yet remained in the hall eating and dancing, Tavis lifted her into his arms and carried her away. From the hall, up the stairs and to the room that would be theirs for the night. Her breath caught as he whispered promises about what his plans were for the two of them. Within minutes, he stood her before him and dropped the door latch, giving them some assurance that they would not be disturbed.

The room looked lovely with flower petals strewn on the bed and the soft light from many candles. A small platter held some special desserts and a bottle of wine awaited them. Ciara poured a cup of the wine for each of them and wondered if she should be nervous.

'You look worried, love,' he said from behind her. He lifted her hair from her shoulders, exposing her neck to him. Remembering the touch of his mouth there, she waited, holding her breath in anticipation of repeating the pleasure.

His mouth was hot as he kissed her along the sensitive skin. He followed it down, unlacing the top of her gown and pushing it off her shoulder so he could taste the curve of her neck there. Part of her wished he would tear her clothes off and finish it while part enjoyed the way he lingered in this one place.

'I am not worried,' she said on a sigh. 'I am just worried.'

He laughed then. 'Worried about what?' His mouth moved up to the tickling spot just beneath her ear and she giggled and shivered as he touched it.

'If I will please you this night,' she admitted.

'If you please me any more than you did that night in my cottage, I will not survive.'

He took the cup from her and placed it back on the table. Holding her against him, she felt proof of his desire against her back and she leaned against it.

'I could restrain myself that night, knowing that you did not belong to me, but now,' he said, kissing her mouth as he turned her in his arms, 'now you are mine.'

She reached up to remove her gown, but he rubbed her arms and placed them at her sides.

'It is my turn to undress you,' he said. The words sounded so scandalous and her stomach tightened with excitement. The place between her legs grew achy and moist as she thought of what was to happen between them.

He untied her laces and eased the gown the rest of the way, sliding it down over her arms and guiding it over her breasts and belly and then her hips until it dropped to the floor. Tavis gave her his hand so she could step from it. He carefully picked it up and draped it over a chair and that pleased her. He turned back and just stared at her, his eyes moving over her flesh and she could almost feel his touch every place that he looked.

Before he took off the chemise, he used the back of his hand to glide over the surface of it, teasing her with the lightest of touches. The tips of her breasts tightened into buds and her breasts felt heavy and ached for more. Her head drifted back and she could feel the length of her hair sliding across her back and legs. She wanted him to touch her, touch her and make her scream in pleasure, but he was taking too long.

'Please,' she whispered. 'Please?'

It was the last thing she said for some time.

He would have gone slowly, but when she begged him, he lost all control. Tavis pulled the chemise off and began to kiss her where she stood. Her mouth beckoned him and he tasted her there first. Hot, open-mouthed kisses that incited him to more. When she was breathless and her mouth well kissed, he traced a path down her neck and shoulders, teasing her breasts with feathery caresses of his tongue until he reached her belly.

Her legs trembled, so he guided her back against the edge of the bed to sit. When she did, he knelt between her legs and gently eased them apart. He knew she'd liked this the first time, but now was his turn to drive her mad. And he would.

Leaning forwards, he kissed the inside of her thighs, waiting for her to relax them. When they fell open wider, he lifted her legs over his shoulders and feasted on her flesh. Holding her hips, he kept her there, licking the heated folds until they wept against his mouth. She sighed, she moaned and she arched against his mouth, but he did not relent.

He slid his tongue deep there and then found the small taut bud that he knew would send her reeling into release. He licked it once, then again when she thrust herself against his mouth. Laughing, he paused for a moment and then took the bud between his teeth and tugged on it gently. She screamed then, tossing and writhing against him, wanting more. So he gave her more, then he listened as everything tight within her body released in a torrent of pleasure. He lifted up and used his fingers to ease the tight opening wider. She gasped over and over as he slid one, then two fingers deep inside her. When she pushed herself against them, he knew it was time.

Tavis did not take the time to undress; he just freed himself from his trews, placed her legs around his hips and eased inside her. He moved deeper as slowly as he could to allow her body to accommodate his. Then, with a final thrust, he claimed her and made them one. Watching her face as his flesh became hers, when there was no ending of his and no beginning of hers, he realised the expression that lay across her features: transcendent. Her face glowed with passion and her eyes were filled with love in that moment. If he had worried about this being the right thing to do, that expression convinced him of the rightness of it. He leaned down and kissed her mouth, gently tasting her as he eased back and then pushed forwards the rest of the way inside her. She wrapped her arms around his and he slid them higher up on to the bed.

He felt her tightness surrounding him and reached down between their bodies to bring her more pleasure. His finger barely touched and she arched against him, causing him to thrust deeper. She moaned. He eased out a bit and then thrust back in, moving slowly so that her flesh grew softer. When she reached down and grabbed his arse, he let go of his control and filled her, claiming every inch of her flesh as his.

She matched his rhythm quickly, lifting her hips to his thrusts.

'Mine,' he whispered over and over against her ear until the waves of pleasure stopped. 'Mine.'

'Yours,' she whispered back.

He remained deep inside her for some time and she could still feel him there, though not as large or as hard as he'd been. Ciara tried to remain still, for it felt wonderful to keep him as part of her flesh, but he shifted his weight off her and separated from her. She felt empty in a strange way that she could not explain.

He slipped from the bed and removed the rest of his clothes. Then he brought a basin and cloth over to the bed and waited for her to use it. The warmth of the rose-scented water helped ease the slight stinging there. But other than that brief, sharp twinge, she had felt only pleasure during their joining. Tavis showed her great care as he helped her from the bed and pulled the covers back. Settling her under them, he climbed back in next to her and took her in his arms.

They lay there in the silence for a few minutes and then she turned to him.

'I wonder where James and Elizabeth are,' she said.

He laughed and kissed her. 'Of all the things you could have said, I did not expect that.'

'She is my closest friend. She should have told me,' Ciara said. 'I was so deep in my own misery that I never saw that she and James were falling in love right in front of me.'

'Must we speak of them right now?' he asked, in a tone that sounded annoyed.

'Is there something else you'd like to talk about?' she asked. 'We are not expected back in the hall until morning.'

He snorted and she looked at him. He didn't look angry, but clearly he was not interested in talking to her.

'I have never done this before,' she admitted. 'I do not know what is proper.'

'Proper?' He rolled her on her back under him and she felt the heat of his body surround hers. 'We are naked, in a bed, married. There is no such thing as proper now.' As if to make his point clearer, she felt him harden against her leg.

'Can we...do we...?' Just that contact excited her, but Ciara was not sure how to ask for what she wanted.

'Ciara, my love,' he whispered to her, 'we can. We do.'

He kissed her then and she forgot all her worries. All the years she'd waited and wanted and hoped and prayed were over. He was hers now and they had their entire lives ahead of them.

And the rest of this night.

Chapter Twenty-Two

Marian could only smile. As did Jocelyn, Margriet and Margaret. Sitting at the high table with their husbands, they all were smiling.

Although the men had doubted that Tavis would ever declare his love for Ciara, the women never had. Over the last several years, as he went through such terrible grief over his loss of Saraid, he never turned from Ciara. Even though something had happened between them, a reckoning of a sort, more than a year ago, he still watched and watched over her, never letting go completely.

And, in spite of agreeing to a number of possible matches and almost going through with this one, Ciara had never stopped loving Tavis.

Marian sighed then and the women all smiled more.

The husbands had a different reaction, though.

Connor shook his head. 'James would have been a suitable husband for her,' he said. The other men shook their heads in agreement... as he knew they would. It was hard for them to lose a wager.

Especially one made to their wives.

'I thought he would let her marry James,' said Rurik. 'Tavis did not seem interested in marrying her, though he wanted her, that was clear.'

'Rurik!' Margriet said. 'He loved her.'

'I do not think he stood a chance against her,' Duncan said. 'She has a way of knowing what she wants and getting it, no matter how long it takes.'

'And you are proud of her,' Marian said. 'Do you think she will continue to help you in your work now that she is married?'

'I think she and Tavis will work things out between themselves,' Duncan said. 'In spite of a strange beginning, I think they will be happy.'

'Well,' Connor said, holding up his cup in

front of them. 'I wish them well,' he said. 'To Tavis and Ciara!'

'To Tavis and Ciara!' they called out.

Marian glanced at the others and reminded them, 'But the proof of who wins our wager will come in a year.'

'By then, your daughter or son will be ready to consider marriage, Jocelyn,' Margriet said.

Jocelyn paled and Connor laughed. ''Tis easier when someone else's bairn is in the middle of it, is it not, love?' he asked, reaching out to stroke his wife's cheek.

'You are right, Connor. They all seem so young to me, even though I know it is nearly time to let them go.'

'If Tavis and Ciara are any indication, I think there is much happiness out there awaiting them all.'

One by one each couple left the high table, heading for their own cottages and beds until only Connor and Jocelyn remained.

'Are you pleased with this match, Connor? Will it cause problems with the contracts and agreements you made with the Murrays?' Jocelyn asked him.

'I think it will all work out—Murray thinks he got out of this with a decent dowry, a more acceptable and suitable wife for his son and an agreement that allies him with our clan. And he did,' Connor explained. 'But we get to keep Ciara where she belongs and Tavis continues in my service where I need him most—here. And we get access to the ports I need to expand our trading business on to the Continent.'

'And you knew all of that would happen?' Jocelyn asked.

'I knew Tavis would not be able to let her marry another. That much was clear even to me.'

Jocelyn laughed and the sound of it brightened his soul. She might think him unable or unwilling to place a value on love, but she forgot that she had taught him the importance of it.

'There might be hope for you yet, Connor,' she said softly, touching his hand and stroking it gently.

'Aye, there just might be.'

And the laird and lady of Lairig Dubh were the last to leave their hall.

Epilogue

Lairig Dubh, Scotland—spring AD 1373

Ciara walked through the small house, touching everything as she did. Each piece of furniture, from the new table to the mantel over the hearth, the chairs and the stools—he had made every piece of it, all of it, just for them.

Tavis had worked for months, crafting the furnishings for their new home in between his duties to the laird; now that it was ready, Ciara just wanted to stand and stare at it all. A labour of love on his part and one she would forever treasure.

She climbed the stairs to the second floor and entered the bedchamber. Even the bed was new and it was wide and high and well-strung. In spite of her loathing of needlework, Ciara, with the help of her mother and Beitris, who excelled at it, had sewn the bedcovers that lay over it now and she reached out to smooth them. A home built with love, she thought as she made her way back down the stairs.

They had decided to accept the laird's invitation to live in the keep until they built a new house. Living in Saraid's house together did not feel right to her and so, using some of her dowry, they planned a new one. And now it was ready.

And just in time.

The last year and a half had sped by for them as they adjusted to married life and being a part of the clan. The laird had asked Ciara to work with her father and use her skills for their benefit and she loved her work. Tavis remained in charge of his personal guard and travelled with the laird when needed or travelled with Ciara and her parents when they carried out the business of the MacLeries.

In slower times, she did teach Tavis to read as she had offered on that day long, long ago and he taught her many, many things. She blushed at the thought of some of them now, but he also taught her how to compromise and to cook. In learning and perfecting other skills, her ability to cook had never been one she practised, until they were about to move into this new home and one where she would be in charge of such matters. She had not revealed that she had hired someone to help her keep house and to watch over things when they were not home.

The door opened and she heard his footsteps behind her. His hands slid around her and came to rest on her large belly.

'You did not carry anything up the stairs, did you?' he asked, nuzzling her neck until she laughed.

'Nay, Tavis,' she replied, turning in his embrace.

'Do you like it?' he asked, releasing her and leading her to a chair. 'Did you see the bedchamber?'

'I did,' she said. ''Tis exactly as I'd hoped.'

Although he pretended not to like to talk and used all sorts of distractions to keep her from too many conversations, they had talked and planned and discussed every inch of the plans for this house before a piece of wood was chopped or a stone moved for it. His ability to carve extended to larger work and not just the small animals made to entertain a child.

Those precious carvings, along with the newest ones, sat on a shelf in the room where their bairn would sleep and would wait for that child to play with them as she had all those years before.

He poured her a cup of watered ale and handed it to her, then sat next to her.

'What did Gunna say?'

'The bairn should be fine, Tavis.'

'And you?'

'I am fine as well. As long as I do not have pains, I can keep up my regular activities.'

'No riding.'

'No riding,' she said with a sigh. 'And no carrying.'

'You will listen to her instructions?' he asked.

'Aye.'

He worried for her. After his experience with Saraid, she was not surprised by it. Though he tried to control it, she knew he watched her more closely as she got further along in carrying their bairn. She would wake up at night and find him lying at her side just watching her sleep.

'All will be well,' she said. She reached up and stroked his cheek, gazing into the green eyes that reflected the love she felt for him. 'I promise it.'

And as they sat together in their new home for the first time, Ciara looked around and realised that everything was there exactly as she had hoped and dreamt it would be when she first claimed Tavis for herself. It had taken her more than ten years to get him, but she was glad she had waited for him as her heart had told her to do.

He was well worth the wait.

* * * * *

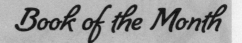

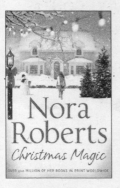

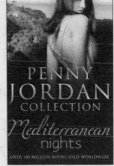